AWAKENING JESSICA

AWAKENING JESSICA

Athena Michaels

This edition first published in the UK in 2014 by
Telos Publishing Ltd, 17 Pendre Avenue, Prestatyn, LL19
9SH

www.telos.co.uk

Telos Publishing Ltd values feedback. Please e-mail us
with any comments you may have about this book to:
feedback@telos.co.uk

ISBN: 978-1-84583-883-6

British Library Cataloguing in Publication Data.
A catalogue record for this book is available from the
British Library.

CONTAINS ADULT CONTENT

PROLOGUE

The dancer moaned with pleasure. Watching from her hiding place, Jessica pressed her hands between her thighs. Her clitoris felt enlarged and swollen with the excitement of catching sight of this illicit rendezvous.

In the next room Leo bent the dancer over a table, kneading her tight buttocks, his fingers massaging between her legs as she squirmed beneath him. Her dress was pushed up above her hips and her hands were clutching the edge of the table as Leo's clever fingers stroked and caressed her. The dancer gasped as he plunged a finger inside her, opening her up for a further invasion.

'Oh Leo …'

'You like that do you? You dirty little bitch …' His laughter was hollow and, Jessica thought, somewhat cynical.

Through the crack in the wall, Jessica watched as with one hand Leo freed his cock from his trousers. It reared up and her eyes widened. He was big. The dancer's muscular legs tensed as Leo positioned himself at her entrance. And with no attempt at subtly or teasing he thrust himself deeply into her.

'Oh my God,' the dancer cried out.

The poor girl, thought Jessica, having all that meat suddenly forced inside her. But her own pussy convulsed at the thought and she lifted her dress and rubbed herself a little to try and still the rising passion there.

In the other room, there was no attempt being made to still any passions as Leo thrust firmly in and out of the dancer. Her moans turned to cries of pleasure and her hands scrabbled at the table as Leo took her fast and deep.

'Leo … Oh yes!'

Leo's breath came faster and louder as the dancer cried out again. He ground himself harder against her bottom, forcing himself deeper inside her from behind. Her face contorted, she seemed torn between both pleasure and pain as she started to orgasm. The girl tried to turn. She reached up to him in an attempt to pull him closer, her mouth opening as she clearly wanted to be kissed. But Leo roughly pushed her back down flat against the table, grunting as he thrust into her, one hand firmly between her shoulder blades. The girl began to scream as her orgasm wracked her whole body. Her legs trembled against the table and as the energy left her limbs she became limp. But Leo showed no mercy as he pounded her harder. His climax was sudden. His bare buttocks tightened as he unloaded his seed deeply into the spasming woman.

Her whimpering quietened as he pulled out, leaving her flat against the table, her breath ragged and weak. Smiling his annoying self-satisfied smile he wiped his cock on her dress and tidied himself away, immediately appearing calm and unruffled.

'Oh my God, Leo,' the dancer had pushed herself up on her arms and was watching him with hooded eyes. 'That was … that was just …'

'Yeah, I know,' he said.

Leo smacked her upturned buttocks. 'Come on then, sort yourself out, rehearsals start in five minutes.'

She stood on shaky legs, and Jessica could only imagine what the aftermath of such an orgasm might be like. A shudder wracked Jessica's body as she shook away the excitement that threatened to engulf her. She couldn't resist massaging her clit a little harder, torturing herself with the unfulfilled need that rose every time she watched Leo and his conquests.

'Give me a moment,' said the dancer. 'Still a little breathless you know.'

Leo grinned again. 'Yeah, whatever,' he said, checking his watch.

The dancer frowned. 'What is it?'

Jessica straightened up; she had seen this sort of exchange before. All the girls Leo gave attention to tended to fall for his roguish charm and his good line in promises. He was, after all, the star of the ballet. A brilliant and talented dancer, with a great body and, she considered, an impressive dick. The problem was that he knew it. And he used all the elements in his arsenal to his advantage as he worked his way through all the girls in the company. All that is, except Jessica, who so far had been ignored by Leo. Probably because her pale skin and long red hair made her look somewhat mousey and uninteresting. She wore her hair pulled back in a severe bun, the way most dancers had it, but this just emphasised her plainness. Jessica knew that she was probably invisible to men like Leo, but that was how she liked it. She would rather not have to find excuses to avoid the advances of a man like him.

In the other room, Leo shrugged. 'We'll be late if

you don't pull yourself together soon.'

'Don't you want to spend some time with me then, Leo?' she purred. 'Is the rehearsal that important?'

Leo looked at her. 'We have spent some time …'

The dancer frowned. 'That quick fuck? You call that some time?'

'Works for me. Now are you coming or what?'

Leo strode from the room, leaving the dancer to try and adjust her dress and retrieve her panties from where they had been thrown underneath the table.

The girl's face was peaked and contorted as she scrambled around trying to compose herself. She had that worried expression they all wore after an encounter with Leo. Well, like all the others she would learn. Jessica wondered how anyone could allow themselves to be treated so badly.

She had never yet seen Leo do anything with any of his conquests that wasn't for his own gratification.

Jessica had stumbled across Leo's favoured liaison point some weeks back. She had been vaguely exploring the basement of the Acadamie where the dancers lived and trained, and had heard noises coming from one of the rooms. She had picked a door at random and found herself in an adjoining room. In the wall there were holes in the plaster and through them she could see quite clearly into the next room where Leo was fucking a dancer whom Jessica recognised as a first year. Because of the darkness, Jessica was well hidden, and the holes were at the right height for her to pull a couch over to lean comfortably against as she watched. Since then Jessica had found herself regularly watching Leo from the shadows. She didn't consider herself to be a peeping tom, but the sight of Leo taking these girls in all manner of ways and positions did arouse her. She told herself, though, that this was arming herself against him, should the invisible girl ever become visible. But really, it had been so long since she herself had made love, the excitement of seeing Leo's trysts had become somewhat addictive.

Jessica had left her long-term boyfriend back in England, over a year ago, when she had first joined the Acadamie. At first her forced celibacy had seemed appropriate. She had to train and work hard to obtain the standard needed to make it through the six months trial period. Now it had almost become a way of life. She was forever on the outskirts, looking in at the passions and intrigues of the other dancers, and particularly Leo. And all this time she never experienced real intimacy herself.

Jessica remained hidden as the dancer followed Leo out. She waited a few more minutes before exiting the room and making her way back upstairs, carefully smoothing her bun to eradicate some imagined tousling. In some small part of her brain, she craved attention, wanted a secret passion, but never would she submit to a man like Leo.

1

As she walked through the impressive hallway, Jessica considered the heritage of the Acadamie. The building itself was stately and quaint, which was what had led her to explore the rooms and levels so thoroughly. Back home in England, she had lived a quiet life in Barnes on the outskirts of London. All she had ever wanted was to dance, and she had worked hard to attain the standard needed to gain entrance to the Acadamie, which was located just outside Rome. Of course it helped that, in common with all the students, she had a rich father who liked to indulge her. Her own dance teacher had followed a successful career in Florence and had trained all of her students in the style the Acadamie de Rousseau preferred. But she had seen right away that Jessica had the talent and passion, and as soon as she had been ready she had encouraged her to audition.

That was 18 months before, just after Jessica had turned 21, and Jessica had successfully gained a place, living and training at the Acadamie. It was her ambition not only to train there, but also to become one of the lead dancers in the Ballet dell Italia attached to the school.

'Stupid girl! Watch where you're going!'

Jessica looked up to see that in her reverie she had nearly walked into a group of girls in the hall. Worse, they were *Natalie's* crowd.

In every school environment there seemed to be a group of girls who clubbed together with the express purpose of making Jessica's life hell. At junior school in Barnes it had been Frankie, Lisa and Marta. At secondary school it was the turn of the truly cruel Simone to make every moment sheer torture, and here it was Natalie.

'I'm sorry,' muttered Jessica, turning and walking quickly away in order to put as much distance between her and the other girls as she could. But their mocking laughter followed her down the hallway as a reminder that there was no safe haven, even in the hollows of the Acadamie, from their persistent cruelty.

Jessica knew what they were saying. That she always had her head in the clouds. That she was hopeless at everything. That she had no boyfriend and was therefore either a lesbian or frigid. Delete as necessary.

Normally this sort of taunt was like water off a duck's back to Jessica, but lately she had been feeling the pressure of there being no man in her life – and she was very sure that a man was what she wanted.

This was all down to Leo of course. Leo the 'magnificent'. She smiled to herself at that thought. She couldn't stand the guy, but that didn't stop him being unbelievably attractive. Leo was the kind of man that women hated but loved; they just couldn't understand why. He was the ultimate bad boy and therefore irresistible to most. But not to her.

As though her thoughts had summoned him, Leo strode down the corridor. He was well built and his dancer's physique rippled under his unitard. At 26, he was a little older than most of the other dancers at the Acadamie; a fact he used to his advantage with many of the young and more impressionable females. He was also the man chosen to dance the lead in most of the ballet's productions and this gave him an ego to match the size of his dick.

Jessica watched as he confidently prowled down the corridor, giving deliberately contrived, sultry looks to the girls as he passed them. He touched some of them on the arm (usually those with whom he had not yet slept), giving sly winks to others (whom he was currently fucking) and totally blanking the increasing number that he had enjoyed and then cruelly discarded.

'Like a peacock, isn't he?' Jessica turned to see Anthony standing behind her.

'I don't know what you mean,' she smiled.

'Right ...'

Anthony was her only real friend at the Acadamie. She had met him on her second or third day there when she had got herself hopelessly lost in the rabbit-warren of corridors and, needing to find her way to the dance hall, had ended up standing pathetically looking at yet another dead end passage.

Anthony had come to her rescue, appearing from nowhere, it seemed, to show her the way back to the hall. He was a stage hand working at the Acadamie, but also seemed to turn his hand to all manner of things that needed doing. He could paint and do carpentry, was a dab hand with a needle and thread, and could mop up spills efficiently. He seemed to be everything from props master to wardrobe mistress, janitor to security guard ... There was nothing he wouldn't do.

Of course, the fact that he kept things moving made him invisible to most of the students. Add to this that he walked with a stick and had a pronounced limp, and he was more often the subject of ridicule from the likes of Leo and Natalie. Jessica had found a kindred spirit. The fact that he was a fellow Brit and she could converse with him in English, rather than the slightly stilted Italian she had to use when talking to most of the other students, only made their bond stronger.

'So what are you up to?' Anthony asked.

'Just mooching,' said Jessica with another smile.

'Sure you're not running?' Anthony asked with a glance at Natalie and her crew, fawning over Leo as he reached their little group. One of the girls seemed to be asking Leo about something on her leg as she had it stretched out and was posing for him *en pointe*. Leo's hand lingered just a little too long on the girl's thigh, and Jessica saw the look, familiar to her now, exchanged between them, which told her that she would be observing Leo and this girl in the downstairs room before very long.

'They'd better watch out,' said Anthony. 'Here comes Rowan.'

'Leo's so-called "official" girlfriend ...'

'The darling of the Acadamie ...' Anthony grinned.

'How she doesn't know what Leo gets up to with the other girls I have no idea,' Jessica said.

'I wouldn't want to be in Leo's shoes if she ever finds out.'

Jessica smiled at Anthony, 'No sympathy? Even for your brother?'

Anthony laughed, leaning casually on his stick. 'What do you think?'

As usual Rowan was wearing a low-cut dance leotard, high cut around the leg so that it clung to and emphasised her slim waist and hips. Over her shoulders she had draped a white silk scarf that set off the yellow of her leotard. Her taut and toned legs were clad in a pair of fishnet tights, and on her feet she had a pair of flat gold slippers. She looked sensual and cat-like as she sashayed down towards Leo.

'Shame she doesn't know the cream in her bowl has gone sour …' Jessica murmured.

Like magic, the girls around Leo evaporated away, as if they had never been there, and he grinned as Rowan approached him,

'Hi babe,' he boomed, loud enough for the whole corridor to hear him.

Rowan air kissed him, but Leo's hand curled around her tiny waist and cupped a perfect buttock for a squeeze.

'Leo! Not here!' Rowan giggled, even though Jessica knew that this was what she loved. Asserting her claim over her man in public.

'What a pair,' said Anthony shaking his head. 'Did you hear about the Acadamie?'

The sudden change of subject didn't surprise Jessica; conversation was always easy with Anthony. They seemed in tune with each other's thought patterns, which was why Jessica knew they made such good friends.

'What about it?' asked Jessica, knowing that Anthony was a good source for gossip that, on occasion, had saved her in tricky one-upmanship contests with some of the girls.

'There's no more money,' said Anthony. 'None at all.'

'But … what does that mean?' asked Jessica, knowing full well that this place was run on grants from various sources as well as the money from the various 'daddies' of the students.

'Seems that the next ballet may be make or break. They're looking to up the ante on all levels for it.'

'But they always say that,' said Jessica. 'Why is this time any different? How do you know?'

'I was clearing out some filing cabinets in one of the rooms adjoining the principal's office yesterday,' said Anthony. 'And some of those money men have very loud voices.' He smiled conspiratorially.

Jessica considered the information. It was certainly true that there seemed to be a lot riding on the next production. There was a casting for it that very afternoon in fact, but it was almost a given that Leo and Rowan would take the leads. As usual.

'Best get back to work … One day they may even miss me!'

Anthony disappeared off down the corridor, his stick, as usual, helping him along.

Jessica watched him go. A twinge pulled at her insides momentarily. She knew exactly what he meant; it was almost as if Anthony was as invisible as she was. She couldn't understand it at all, of course. He was a lovely man, probably around 30, with a shock of brown hair and twinkling blue eyes. He was always smiling, despite the limp and the stick, always happy and always very approachable. That aside, if he wasn't her friend she might even have said he was very attractive. And he was, too, on many levels; charismatic in a shy, unassuming way. Not in the least like his brother Leo. It was hard to believe that he and Leo were indeed brothers, their nature was so different, but Jessica could see the similarity in their build and in their eyes.

Jessica was roused from her reverie by the sight of Marco, another student at the Acadamie. Instinctively

Jessica pulled her stomach in a little and thrust her breasts out farther. She liked Marco. A lot.

Marco smiled at her as he passed and she smiled back. He had a warm smile, not false or predatory but genuine and kind. But Jessica, being Jessica, had never spoken to him. She was afraid he would reject her, or worse, that it would turn out that he already had a girlfriend. Then news of her hopeless attraction would spread around the students like wildfire and the other girls would have all the ammo they needed in order to make her life more miserable. Then she was certain to become even more introverted.

Jessica sighed and checked the time on her mobile phone. It was five minutes to her next lesson.

Bloody Hell. Deportment with Miss Mathias, she thought. An hour of torture holding your body in unnatural poses that were supposed to aid gracefulness on stage.

Oh well. Nothing to do but go with the flow. Jessica headed off to the lesson, once more becoming the invisible girl as she threaded her way through the other students in the corridor.

2

'Oh Leo …'

Jessica smiled as she leaned against the couch in the lower room. Time for some more entertainment.

'Are you sure this is safe?'

Jessica recognised the girl as the one from the corridor not two hours earlier. Leo worked fast!

'Course it's safe, Yvonne …'

'It's Yvette …'

'Yeah, whatever … Now come here …'

Leo drew the pretty brunette to him and kissed her, hungrily. She responded and snaked one hand around the back of his neck to return the kiss.

Jessica wondered at the difference between them. Leo must have been around six foot tall, but Yvette was barely five. Many of the dancers were very petite indeed; pretty little dolls with perfectly proportioned bodies, able to buy their clothes from the junior rails at the shops if they so pleased. Jessica hated them all. She was a little on the lanky side for a dancer at five foot six, but this height gave her a gracefulness that she knew many of the others lacked. Maybe this was why they dismissed her.

Yvette giggled as Leo caressed her body through the tight lycra of her leotard. Jessica had to suppress a whistle. The girl was stunning. Curves in all the right places and Leo certainly knew how to appreciate them.

She was running her hands down his muscled torso now, feeling the hard body. Leo smiled, and started to strip his own unitard off, revealing a nearly hairless body. Yvette had reached his crotch and was stroking there with one hand, feeling the growing length of his cock as he stiffened from the attention.

Seeing that his top half was now uncovered, Yvette moved her attention to his nipples and stroked them gently with her thumbs before dipping her head slightly to lick and then suck on them alternately. Leo's head threw back, his eyes closed, and he groaned a little as he allowed her to pleasure him.

A moment later he pushed his unitard completely off, freeing his throbbing cock, which was growing larger and stiffer with every second.

He stroked the back of Yvette's head, displaying uncharacteristic affection. She relaxed into him, completely compliant as he started to slide the tight leotard off her shoulders and down her body. Once it pooled around her feet, he stepped back to take in Yvette in all her glory.

Her breasts were a little on the large side for a dancer, stiffly peaked with tight pink nipples, her waist was small and her hips perfect. She was wearing a tiny black thong, the material of which vanished between her ass cheeks from Jessica's position.

Leo was certainly impressed. His cock jerked and bounced as Yvette did a little twirl for him.

'Like it?' she asked.

'Very much,' he grunted, reaching out to her.

She looked at him coyly. 'So when is the casting for the next production?'

Here it comes, thought Jessica … This is where the promises and lies start. Where Leo plays his games.

There was a sound in the room behind Jessica and she froze.

She had definitely heard something. A gentle movement as though a foot had scraped against something.

She peered around slowly. Everything was silent and still in the darkness. She could hear the muffled sounds from the next room, but there was nothing else.

She carefully shifted her position to look around. Nothing. The room was inky black and she couldn't see in all the corners, but she thought she was okay.

She shook her head, and returned her attention to the scene in the next room.

Leo had stopped talking and was slowly nodding his head while breathing heavily.

Yvette had also stopped talking as she had several inches of rock-hard cock buried half way down her throat.

Jessica watched in amazement as the little dancer sucked Leo's cock like some professional whore, taking it really deep, and then sliding it out, all the while stroking the shaft with her small hands and teasing the underside of Leo's balls as she did so.

Jessica knew that Leo liked this sort of attention, and would, if he could, get the girls to go down on him at every opportunity. But Yvette, it seemed, had some talent in this department, and Leo was relishing it.

'I always recommend a girl who has talent …'

Yvette's eyes widened slightly and she renewed her worship of Leo's cock with increased fervour. Leo groaned, his hips moving faster as he fucked Yvette's mouth.

Jessica wondered, not for the first time, what it might be like to have a man's cock in her mouth. What would it taste like? Salty like some of the girls said, or sweet like some others claimed. How could you deep throat something so big without gagging? And what would it feel like erupting in your mouth and down your throat?

Yvette obviously knew, and was sucking on Leo like her life depended on it; clearly she thought her career did. Leo was moaning softly now, bracing himself against the table as Yvette worked magic on his cock and balls, kneeling before him and worshipping him.

Leo's moans rose in volume and he ran his hands through Yvette's hair as she worked him faster. He yanked on her hair, pulling her head down on him harder.

With a cry, Leo shuddered, and his face creased as he started cumming into Yvette's mouth. Jessica was doubly impressed. Sometimes when the girls got this far, they pulled away too soon, not wishing to have Leo's seed in their mouth, but the inevitable result was that it then went all over their face and hair. Not that Leo cared of course.

But Yvette. What a trooper. She continued sucking as Leo moaned and thrashed, and drained his balls of every drop before letting his clean cock emerge from her mouth with a plopping sound.

'So how was that?' said Yvette coyly, obviously having swallowed Leo's cum as though starved of protein.

'Fucking hell,' was all Leo could say. 'That was amazing.'

Jessica assumed that Yvette smiled – she couldn't see her face from this angle – and watched as the girl gracefully rose to her feet and caressed Leo's still hard manhood in her hand.

Leo shook his head. 'Have to be next time babe.'

'Okay.'

Yvette didn't even seem fazed by this dismissal. But then she turned and Jessica saw her face watching Leo. She was rapt, as though she had just been servicing her God, her lord, her master.

'Oh dear. She has it bad,' Jessica whispered under her breath.

Sooner or later one of these obsessive types was going to be the ruin of Leo.

Leo smiled at Yvette and helped her back on with her leotard, taking every opportunity to stroke and caress her naked breasts and body in the process. Then he quickly donned his own outfit and held the door for her. It was only later in their relationships that the girls came to realise what a slimeball Leo really was. At the start he was like the perfect gentleman.

After Leo and Yvette had left, Jessica sat and waited her usual five minutes, and just as she was about to go, she again heard the furtive scraping noise from behind her. She whirled to look, wondering if it was a rat or something, but again, there was nothing there.

From the corner of her eye she caught a movement as something quickly left the room. Something man-sized. She leaped to the door, which was swinging closed, and looked out into the corridor. She caught a glimpse of a person hurrying away from her, dressed in black. There was something wrong with the figure's face though, and when he reached the corner, he looked back at her before vanishing from sight.

Although she had caught only the briefest of glimpses, Jessica realised that the figure had been wearing a mask. The feelings that swirled inside her were somewhere between fear and arousal. Strange, but the thought of someone watching her, watching Leo, was sexy and she couldn't shake the surge of lust that rushed through her loins as she wondered what this might mean.

3

'The ballet will be presented in three months time,' Madame Rossi explained. 'And as some of you are aware, this time we are presenting something slightly different. In the past, our productions have tended toward the classical, but this time, we have been asked to present something more contemporary. We have with great deliberation decided upon a reworking of Stravinsky's *Appollon Musagete*.'

A collective gasp echoed through the room as the dancers glanced excitedly around at each other.

'Our plan is to modernise the ballet still further. It will bring the Acadamie into the 21st Century and ultimately aid our bid for future sponsorships. Those involved will have to work hard, as the Acadamie demands nothing short of perfection from those who participate!'

Jessica stood at the back. The casting call had been posted on the notice boards around the Acadamie for weeks now, and many of the students had been excitedly training and gearing themselves up to audition for the five main parts in the production.

I know I'm ready, Jessica thought. But deep down, a

nagging doubt paralysed her and she felt unable to move forward to draw the Madame's attention to her. There were so many good dancers here; no way would they take a mousy redhead for any respectable part. She would be lucky to make the Chorus …

Jessica shook her head in a subconscious gesture to quiet the nagging voice.

At the front of the room, Madame Rossi finished her introduction, and her eyes swept around the room. As usual Leo was standing near the front, chest puffed out, ready for whatever challenges might come his way. He was smiling to himself. Just behind him, Yvette stood among the crowd of friends who made Jessica's life miserable. She looked like the proverbial cat that had got the cream, but her features were tinged with something between arrogance and desperation. She licked her lips subconsciously, as though recalling the taste of Leo, and she glanced at him furtively every few minutes.

'So now then, ladies and gentlemen,' said Madame Rossi, her Italian accent strong, 'it is time to see who wants to audition for the production …'

She smiled at her charges.

'First, we have the leads.'

Leo's smile widened at the words, and he stepped forward. 'Madame.'

'Yes of course, Leo,' the woman said, 'You will of course take the part of Apollo.'

Leo nodded with satisfaction.

'And for Calliope …' continued Madame Rossi.

Jessica looked around. Where was Rowan? There was no sign of her in the room, and the Acadamie rules said that if you wanted to be part of the productions then you had to attend the castings. No exceptions. The basis being that to appear required dedication, reliability and punctuality, so if you didn't show at the casting, then you could not be considered.

'… the first female lead …' said Madame Rossi, casting her eyes over the assembled students.

There was a shifting of feet, and some girls looked expectantly at the Madame, many hoping to be selected to audition and have an opportunity to carry the production with Leo. Although deep down each of them knew that they had no chance of anything above a small part.

Jessica was in turmoil. She believed she could do this, she knew the part, had been studying it since the production had been announced, but did she have what it took?

Looking around at the other girls, she was on the verge of making up her mind. On the verge of raising her hand. In her mind's eye she saw herself doing just that, stepping forward and saying in a clear voice, 'I will audition for that part, Madame Rossi.'

'I will take that part Madame Rossi.'

Jessica frowned. Had she said that out loud?

No. The voice came from the back of the room. And there, lounging casually against the wall was … bloody Rowan.

She pushed herself away from the wall and sauntered confidently through the other students to the front of the studio. She moved gracefully, her pale blue unitard showing her well-defined physique.

'Madame Rossi,' she greeted the teacher.

Rossi smiled a short, hard smile. 'Thought for a moment you weren't going to make it Rowan,' she said.

'Oh, you know me,' replied Rowan, with a crafty wink towards Leo. 'I wanted to give someone else the opportunity to offer to audition. I so hate to think that it is always me in the limelight … However, since no-one else is willing to come forward, then of course you can always rely on me.'

'Ever the manipulator,' whispered Jessica under her breath, as the room relaxed in a silent sigh. The pressure was now on Leo and Rowan to deliver, and as they had done this several times before, the Acadamie was happy that everything was in place.

Jessica let her mind wander, gazing at the large windows in the room and out into the summer sunshine beyond. Why was she wasting her time here? What was there for her, really? She needed a boyfriend. A man in her life. A lover. She sighed. Maybe one day. Maybe sometime.

'Jessica?'

So far she had been disappointed with the men available, but there was going to be a new intake soon. Maybe then there would be someone she could really bond with.

'Jessica?'

Of course there was always Marco … Mmmmm. Lovely Marco with his perfect body and radiant smile. Maybe he … Now there was a sensual possibility.

'Jessica Thomson?'

The sound of her name being called shocked her out of her thoughts. That was her name … She blinked. Madame Rossi and the rest of the class were looking at her.

She felt the blush begin at her neck and her cheeks glowed.

'Yes Madame? Sorry Madame.'

Madame Rossi frowned kindly. 'Seems we need something to keep your mind engaged, Miss Thomson.'

Jessica wanted the floor to open up and swallow her. She nodded sheepishly.

'Miss Thomson,' continued Madame Rossi. 'I know you like to hide in the shadows …'

At this Jessica felt a bubble of panic rise up. Oh my God! She *had* been seen in the basement, and now it had been reported and she was for it. Shit!

'… at the back of class, but I have seen what you are capable of.'

Jessica frowned in confusion. No. Not about the basement rendezvous. But then what?

'So, I'd like to see you audition to understudy Rowan for this part.' Madame Rossi's tone brooked no argument.

Jessica felt her jaw hang free. Understudy the lead? Her?

She found her voice after a few seconds, even though it seemed like an eternity. 'Thank you, Madame.'

Still beside the Madame, Rowan stiffened. 'But Madame, I thought Natalie might …'

Madame Rossi ignored her and continued with the schedule. 'Now, the other roles …'

Jessica wandered to the back of the pack now clamouring to gain the roles of the various dancers and subsidiary characters in the production. Understudy. Wow.

Later she found herself beside Marco by the wall. He was shortlisted for the part of Hades: a good prominent role with lots of potential to flex his abilities on stage.

'Well done,' he whispered.

She felt herself blush again. 'Thanks,' she muttered back. She could hardly believe he had spoken to her.

'You'll be fine,' Marco said. 'First time going for understudy, is it?'

Jessica nodded.

Marco smiled. 'I remember my first time. Terrifying. On the first rehearsal I managed to spill coke all down my unitard and so had this massive stain all over the crotch and down one leg.'

Jessica looked at him wide-eyed.

Marco nodded. 'No-one would believe what had happened. They all thought I had had an accident of another kind.'

He chuckled, and Jessica smiled with him.

'See, not so bad, is it?'

'No,' she admitted.

'Jessica, isn't it?'

She nodded.

'Marco. Marco Dagostino.' He held out his hand to her.

She gripped it. He was cool to the touch. A tiny thrill tickled the insides of her stomach. She never wanted to let go.

'Thanks Marco,' she said.

'Well, good luck,' he said. 'See you at rehearsal.'

'Thanks.'

Jessica watched as Marco drifted off out of the room and on to his next lesson. Well, that's a turn up for the books, she thought. He does know who I am! She smiled to herself. Maybe this term would not turn out to be hopeless after all.

4

Jessica arrived at her next class. She could see that several of the girls were eyeing her. Had they heard already that Madame Rossi had given her the understudy role? Were they envious?

Whatever, that wasn't really her problem. She smiled to herself and started her warm-up on the bar along the wall.

Concentrating hard on getting her leg muscles in tone, Jessica stood *en pointe*, performing a series of complicated exercises designed to strengthen her ankles. Satisfied, she stretched her slender leg up, placing her heel on the high bar. She leaned forward, gracefully stretching out her arm to reach her ankle, increasing the stretch of her inner thigh. Suddenly she was pushed hard from behind. Her leg slipped, something shifted, and she felt an agonising pain blossom in her hip.

'Fuck! Oh shit, fuck!' she mumbled as she fell to the floor.

The girls around her were as usual ignoring her, and there was no sign of whoever had pushed her.

Through tears of pain she thought she saw Natalie smirking a few yards away. She cradled her hip in her hands and tried to stand but the pain seared through her body.

'Miss, miss?'

Natalie's self-satisfied voice called out.

'Miss, Jessica seems to be having some … difficulty.'

'Thank you Natalie,' said Miss Johns, an efficient Englishwoman and an ex-ballerina herself.

'Jessica? What seems to be the trouble?' Miss Johns hurried to her side.

'It's my hip, miss. I think I've strained something.'

Miss Johns indicated a nearby chair. 'Come, sit here.'

She helped Jessica over to sit down.

'And the rest of you,' Miss Johns addressed the class, who had stopped their initial exercises and were now watching the drama unfold. 'Get back to your work.'

With a low mutter the girls returned to their *plié* and stretches, as the piano player started the strains of one of the movements from *Swan Lake*.

'Now Jessica,' said Miss Johns. 'What happened?'

Jessica glanced up and saw that Natalie was still looking at her with evil in her expression. 'I … I don't know. I was warming up and my hip just … It just popped.'

Miss Johns felt carefully around Jessica's upper leg and hip, noting where the girl winced as she encountered the tender area.

'I think you've just strained a muscle my dear. Get yourself to the fitness clinic and they'll sort you out.'

Jessica nodded. She stood up and tenderly hobbled out of the room. She could walk, the pain was easing slightly, but if the injury turned out to be a bad one there was no way that she would be able to dance or even train for several weeks. As she made her way down the corridor toward the clinic she reflected on the disaster area that was her life. How absolutely typical that this would happen, just as she got her first break. She hated herself, hating the teachers, the other girls, the whole Acadamie. She didn't even bother to wipe away the tears that poured down her face as she limped away from the rest of the students.

In the fitness centre, she tried to relax as the physiotherapist massaged her hip, moving her limbs in painful ways.

'It's not as bad as it seems …' Dr Solis concluded. 'It's a minor strain. A few weeks and you can begin to work again. Until then, these are the only exercises you can do. No major dancing. Okay?'

'But …'

'I know it's hard for you girls; the pressure here to sustain your standard by training six hours a day. But believe me when I tell you, a little rest will gain you more than pushing yourself too hard. I know you gained understudy. Congratulations, you deserve it. I'll speak to the Madame. I'm very certain in a few short weeks you'll be able to train again and will be fit and ready for the production.' With that Dr Solis began writing up her medical notes.

Jessica left the centre with a bottle of painkillers and headed back to her room, unable to shake the worry she was feeling despite the doctor's reassurance.

Back in her room, she switched on her mobile phone to see if she had any messages from home. And while she contemplated the phone call she would have to make to her father, her phone vibrated as an incoming text lit up the screen.

'WHY NOT WATCH THE REHEARSAL FROM THE BALCONY?'

Jessica was intrigued. She didn't recognise the number. And when she dialled it, it went through to a generic answer message that gave nothing but a mechanical pre-recording: 'The person you've called is unavailable …'

She stared at her phone for a long time. It wasn't really a surprise that someone she didn't know had her number. All the students' numbers tended to be posted up for all manner of things on the notice boards, and this wasn't the first time she had received a random text from persons unknown.

Her mind turned back to the stranger who had been watching her in the basement … This was all getting very interesting.

There was a thump from the room next door and Jessica's heart fell. Her neighbour there often had friends over to visit, and when they did, they always kept her awake at night.

She checked her watch. It was early for them, but Jessica realised that she was exhausted and so lay down on her bed to rest for a moment.

She heard giggling from the adjoining room and groaned. She was getting fed up of being alone while all around her people got together and had sex.

She heard the bed next door squeak gently as two people got onto it. She imagined she could hear them kissing and the rustle of clothing as eager hands removed it.

Then the girl moaned.

It wouldn't have been so bad, but Cath was a bit of

a squealer when it came to sex. Sometimes Jessica just wanted to bang on the wall herself and shout at her to *shut the fuck up!*

Jessica could hear Cath moaning more loudly now as her partner did something to her. Jessica could only wonder what that was. She pressed her hands down to her crotch and lay there, listening, as the sounds Cath was making got a little louder.

Then they stopped, and Jessica found herself straining to hear the next part of the symphony.

The bedsprings creaked, and then, there it was, the faint tapping of the headboard against the wall. Slow at first, but increasing in tempo.

Jessica could imagine the man, completely naked, on top of Cath. His hard cock pounding into her as she lay, legs spread, enjoying every second.

The headboard started to knock against the wall a little louder.

Why didn't they move the bed away from the wall? Jessica wondered. *Surely that was an obvious thing to do.* Maybe they liked torturing her like this though.

The sounds stopped and Jessica heard more giggling, then a sharp crack. Jessica wondered what that was, but then the image of Cath on her hands and knees came to her. The man positioned behind her about to ravage her little pussy with his big member. The crack was his hand slapping her rump, letting her know who was boss before he started.

Cath cried out in pleasure, and the rhythmic sounds started up again, occasionally punctuated by the slapping sound.

Her moans increased in volume, and Jessica squirmed as her neighbour was rapidly brought to orgasm by whoever was with her.

Cath screamed as she came, and Jessica felt a small shudder run through her own body in response.

The sounds from the next room died away, and Jessica closed her eyes. She had to get a man soon … This was driving her insane.

She checked her watch and saw that 20 minutes had gone by. She had to get ready, and as that strange text had suggested, the balcony overlooking the theatre might be an interesting place to visit.

Slowly she changed from her leotard into a loose and comfortable dress of pale blue satin. Part of her mind insisted that the mystery of who had sent the message was irrelevant. Watching from the balcony would give her a good vantage point, and it was a very good idea for her to keep abreast of the dance moves Rowan would be learning.

She pulled on some pale brown hold-ups and a thong underneath the dress. She was damp from listening to Cath, and she felt strangely excited; maybe the masked stranger would also be on the balcony. Her heart beat a little faster at the thought. From what she had seen, he had a very muscular body. And with the agility he'd demonstrated as he hurried from the room, clearly a dancer's physique.

What's wrong with me? She glanced at her phone again, lying on her bed. Maybe the stranger was Marco? Straightening and automatically brushing down her clothing she slipped on a pair of flat shoes.

A few moments later Jessica gingerly climbed the steep staircase to the balcony overlooking the stage. Madame Rossi had insisted that the dancers abandon the rehearsal rooms in favour of working solely on the stage from the start of the rehearsals. The piece being performed had minimalistic sets, and it was important that the cast learn and understand the spaces they were to work in as well as the moves and the flow of the piece.

Halfway up the steps she paused, rubbing her hip as it ached from the extra exertion. She stood in the dark, listening to the sounds echo up from the stage as Madame Rossi called out instructions to the choral dancers. When the pain in her hip subsided, Jessica once more began to climb the stairs.

The balcony was deserted and silent. She limped across to the farthest corner. Here she could see all the stage, but she could not be seen from below as the area was wreathed in shadows. Leaning against the rail to rest her hip, she looked down. Below, the choral dance rehearsal had just finished. The dancers were gathered together as Madame Rossi gave them notes. Rowan and Leo sat in the stalls below the stage with Marco, who was taking pictures of the proceedings. Marco was sometimes used as photographer for the productions, capturing images that could be distributed to the press. He had a good eye and managed to get the most from the colourful costumes and settings when appropriate. Of course, he also didn't charge anything, which was ideal from the Acadamie's point of view.

'Rowan, Leo,' Madame Rossi boomed, and her voice echoed strangely around the balcony. 'We need to see the love duet.'

Leo stood slowly, holding out his hand to Rowan in an uncharacteristically polite way. But of course, Jessica had seen this behaviour before, and it was obvious that Leo, like the professional he was, was stepping into his role as devoted lover. He was tuning into the emotion that the dance would need. Rowan responded to this, less by design but with the same focus, and Jessica had to admit they did look great as they walked gracefully up onto the stage.

Marco also stood and vanished backstage, perhaps to take some pictures from there? Jessica smiled as he went. She would love to pose for him one day.

As the music started and the dancers took their first positions, Jessica felt the hair stand up on the back of her neck. She loved the ballet and the music always did that to her. As she watched she became engrossed in the rhythms of the music and movement below, mentally walking herself through the steps. She had to remember them, learn them, without actually being able to practice them.

'Don't turn around.'

Jessica froze. Icy strands of fear rippled up her spine.

The voice was soft and whispered and came from behind her.

'I won't hurt you.'

Jessica kept her eyes fixed on the stage below as Leo and Rowan twirled into an embrace. Leo stroked the side of Rowan's face with the palm of one hand before she bounced away in an impressive movement. Jessica could feel her heart pounding.

For a moment she couldn't move. 'Y-you sent the text?'

'Yes,' the whispered voice replied.

She waited for more but the silence was deafening. She started to turn her head to see.

'Don't look.' The whispered command was forceful.

'Who are you?'

'Someone who can help you. Teach you. Better than anything those two can do below.'

'Then why can't I see you?' Jessica half turned

again, caught a glimpse of a tall and strong physique.

'I said don't look!'

Her head snapped back to face front again. Her breathing was coming in short gasps.

'That's good. Don't worry, Jessica. I won't hurt you.'

She closed her eyes and let her breathing return to normal.

She heard a soft rustle behind her and felt, rather than saw, the stranger move closer to her.

She stiffened as she felt a warm hand gently touch her shoulder. The fingers were soft and gentle.

'You are so beautiful, Jessica. You deserve this chance to shine. To prove what you are capable of.'

As the voice whispered, so the fingers stroked across her back, gently kneading her flesh.

Although a small voice was ringing an alarm in her mind, she felt her body respond to the touch. It had been oh so long since she had been touched by a man. And it felt good.

She shuddered and let her breath out in a gasp.

'How can I trust you?' she asked.

Silence. His hands slid over the tops of her arms, nails gently scraping along her bare skin with erotic slowness. She shuddered and her skin dimpled with goose bumps.

'Keep watching below. See how they dance.'

The hands stroked down her waist and nipped her there gently before continuing over the swell of her hips and down her legs. The soft silk of her dress whispered against her flesh.

'How can I ...' she started to say as the hands sensuously stroked around her legs, the bare flesh of her thighs suddenly being in contact with warm fingertips.

Jessica looked at the stage, barely registering what was happening there as her entire world contracted to the sensation of fingers stroking across her thighs between her legs. She felt her womb clench and warmth flood her as the sensations continued.

'You are a beautiful dancer,' the stranger whispered. 'You have an innate sensuality, but you lack the capacity to let go, to give yourself completely to the music.'

The music swelled. Leo and Rowan seemed like ghosts. Their flexible limbs floated over the stage. Jessica felt hypnotised. *Maybe I've been drugged*, she thought.

She unconsciously moved her legs apart, giving the stranger more room in which to stroke her. She could feel his fingers moving higher to her centre. Oh, she wanted to be touched there so much. To feel fingertips gently stroking across her.

'Jessica ...' the stranger whispered and she stiffened, afraid again. 'Tell me to stop and I will.'

Silence. The longest sensual pause that would decide whether she would continue on this path or stop. His fingers found her, skimming over the front of the satin thong. She gasped, pressing herself back against him instinctively. She felt his hardness. His longing, his need, all so very obvious as he ground himself slightly against her upturned bottom.

'Shall I stop?'

Her head was reeling. All she knew was that she wanted this. Needed this. The blood was rushing in her head and the stage seemed like a million miles away.

'No.'

There. She had said it.

She felt gentle fingers finally explore around and over her. They hooked into the material of her thong, and she felt the gentle touch of silk against her thighs as the flimsy underwear was eased down, exposing her.

His fingers slipped around and brushed across her furry mons and rubbed her clitoris gently. She tried to stifle the groan that escaped her lips.

She shifted her legs slightly, wincing as her hip twinged.

'You hurt yourself,' the stranger whispered, his clever fingers touching her sore hip. 'That will soon heal.'

As he spoke, his hands moved around her again, touching her back, her body. His fingers left trails of fire where they moved and she felt herself shudder once more, the pleasure slowly growing.

Silk skirts shifted against her legs, and as she gazed at Leo and Rowan on the stage, she felt a gentle breath of cool air on her thighs as the material was lifted up to expose her. Fingers ran around her hips and down between her legs once more, teasing her and opening her up.

One finger dipped inside her. Oh, she was so wet. She moaned gently, settling herself on the balcony a little more comfortably, taking some weight off her legs onto her arms.

She felt movement behind her and the stranger's hands fell away for a few moments. She could imagine in her mind's eye him freeing himself. After a moment she felt his hardness pressed bare against her, and she found herself arching her bottom, suddenly wanting him inside her.

'Do you want me?' His whispered breath caressed her neck.

'Yes ...'

His hand reached down. It had been so long, the

anticipation now made her pussy ache. She pushed back against him, wanting, needing. Desperation now colouring her every movement. She felt the tip of his cock rub against her entrance teasingly, spreading the wetness that leaked from her. He stroked her bare buttocks, caressing the skin as his cock gently touched her, making her moisten in anticipation. And then his gentle fingers opened her slightly as he pushed forward, lodging the head of his cock just inside her. Jessica fought the urge to impale herself and failed. She sucked air in through her teeth and pushed back, but his hands were now holding her hips.

'No,' he said. 'I want this time to be slow.'

She almost swooned with lust, resting her head on her hand on the rail of the balcony. Down on the stage, oblivious to what was happening above, Leo and Rowan were having some argument about the way the dance was progressing.

The stranger moved Jessica slightly, opening her legs more for ease of entry, and then he began to move.

Jessica bit her hand.

On the stage Rowan was saying something to Leo, posturing.

On the balcony, Jessica felt herself slowly filled as the man pushed forward. She felt the size of him, knew he was big, possibly as big as Leo.

Leo was saying something back, but Jessica didn't care as the stranger's huge cock opened her gently at first, and then slowly started to thrust into her. All of her resistance was driven away by the movement. She was now impaled to the hilt. She could feel his hardness deep inside as he paused to let her come to terms with the sensation. She pushed back, the pain in her hip forgotten as he, this masked stranger, gave her what she had needed for so long.

His strokes were long and agonisingly slow. She felt herself filled to the brim and then an intense feeling of anticipation just before she was filled again. And again. And again.

With each gentle stroke her gasps matched him, breathing in and out in time with him. Whether he was matching her rhythm or she was moving with him she neither knew nor cared. All sensation was being focused into her pussy and deep inside as she could feel his cock touching places that had not been stimulated for so long.

She opened her eyes wide, barely seeing the stage and those on it as the gentle hands on her hips urged her back and forth on the large cock, sliding wetly in and out of her. She felt herself tighten as tiny shocks vibrated through her body.

The stranger continued to stroke long and hard and deep within her. The tension was building. She felt her hands tighten on the balcony rail. Breath coming in short gasps. The deep shocks thrumming through her merged and started on the path leading inexorably towards an orgasm.

'Don't stop …' she murmured. 'Yes …'

The man continued his rhythmic movements.

Jessica moaned gently again as the movements started to peak for her.

Suddenly she was there.

She came hard; pushing back on his cock as she spasmed.

She pushed her mouth against her hand, holding tightly onto the rail, to stifle the moan of pleasure. Her legs shook. The spasms took her body and she came again, harder than before. Now the stranger was all but holding her up as he moved slowly and deeply inside her convulsing body.

Already she was convinced that the sounds of sex would carry down to the stage, but this added to the excitement. The thought of being seen like this was a huge turn-on for her. She shuddered again against him as he slowed slightly, letting her recover. She thought he might pull out then, but instead he increased his movements once more. Slightly faster this time.

She came again.

Jessica could not believe it. She had never before cum twice, let alone … and this third time was exquisite. She squeezed her eyes closed and moaned again. Almost blacking out with the electric shocks that seemed to connect all parts of her body. From her tender breasts to her clitoris, from the sensitive skin below her ears to the backs of her legs, from deep within her to some primal part of her brain that told her that she was being sexed so well …

Then he came inside her, breathing hard as he rocked against her bottom, filling her with his seed. She felt the warmth flood her, bathing her in a sensuous pleasure.

The shocks subsided as he slowed.

'Oh my God,' she murmured.

Her knees were weak. Now she knew how it felt to be taken, to be pleasured so much you could barely stand. And for the first time she realised the addiction of Leo, why the other girls craved more once they'd been with him. And she knew, no matter what, whoever this stranger was, she would want this again. And nothing was going to get in her way.

'I'll be in touch,' he whispered, running his hand over her back.

'Sure you will,' Jessica's heart sank as her

breathing returned to normal. *How stupid I've been!*

'I meant what I said. I can teach you so much about yourself ...'

His hands released her. Her dress fell, covering her buttocks. She tensed herself on her hands. Letting her shaking legs take her weight once more.

'I won't disappoint you, Jessica.'

She felt a kiss placed on the nape of her neck.

She breathed deeply. Down on the stage, the music had started again. The argument, whatever it had been about, was now over, and Leo was trying to perfect a fairly complex jump. Trying the same three steps, hop, spin and land over and over again.

'When will I see you again?' she asked.

There was no reply, and Jessica waited for a beat before turning around slowly. He was gone. Just like that, she thought.

'Hello?' she breathed the question into the darkness of the balcony. But there was no movement and no reply.

Her heartbeat returning to normal, and feeling incredibly satisfied and languid, feeling a slow drip of cum slip down the inside of her thighs, she turned and looked over the balcony at Rowan and Leo. Unable to move, Jessica watched dumbly. She felt drained but elated.

A movement to one side caught her eye. Marco slid into the stalls, his camera in his hand.

Jessica looked down and smiled to herself. Could it be that Marco was her mysterious benefactor? Whoever it was, he certainly knew how to perform. And she found that she was looking forward to the next lesson.

5

Jessica thought that she was becoming obsessed by her phone. She was checking it ever five minutes or so to see if there was another message from the stranger. But there wasn't. And in any case, the phone would vibrate if a message arrived.

Jessica sighed and checked the screen again. Nothing. At this rate she would never get any work done.

During the day, at class, she couldn't check. There was a strict rule that all mobile phones be turned off and left in the students' lockers during the sessions. Sensible but frustrating. Even though Jessica could not take part due to her injury, she still had to attend, and to practice what she could.

So Jessica would get through the classes, trying not to think back to her liaison on the balcony and to concentrate on what the teachers were saying.

Her tight pussy being slowly filled with a thick cock from behind.

She shook her head and massaged her hip.

She tried a *plié* and winced as her leg ached in response. Slow but sure, that was what the doctor had instructed.

She had got through the day, checking her phone after every lesson, only to find nothing there. Now the day was over and she was back in her room. Trying to relax and read again the book for *Appollon Musagete*. She was determined to know it inside and out so that when her hip was better, and the rehearsals really got under way, she would be in the best position to take over the lead should that be required.

Jessica wandered into her bathroom and started to run a bath. Relaxing in some hot, steamy water would be just the ticket.

As it filled, she headed back into her room and stripped off her leotard and leggings. She stood in front of her full-length mirror and examined her body critically. She was not fat, far from it, but she didn't like the way her stomach puffed slightly. She was also critical of her waist – one side seemed to be slimmer than the other. And no-one should get her started on the state of her feet.

She pressed gently on her hip and felt the sting of pain as she touched the healing nerves there. There was a slight greenish tinge to the skin where the bruising was starting to show. But it was getting better. That was the important thing.

She returned to the bathroom and turned off the water. The room was full of steam and the bath brimmed invitingly with bubbles.

With a sigh she lowered herself into the water and lay back.

There were few things in life more pleasurable than soaking in a hot bath, she thought, and closed her eyes.

Gentle fingers caressing her back as a firm cock thrust

into her again and again.

Jessica smiled and trailed her fingers through the hot water.

Cumming hard on a big dick rammed inside her.

Her mind replayed her experience on the balcony again and again. She could feel the soft stroking of fingers on her thighs. Sense the steady breathing of the stranger as he burrowed into her body, bringing her to the heights of passion.

She tensed her legs in the steaming water, and her hand stroked down her flat stomach to where hair tufted and sprang around her sensitive pussy. She rubbed gently, feeling the hair between her fingers.

She was feeling wicked.

Jessica reached over for the shave gel on the side of the bath, and also for her razor. She regularly shaved under her arms, but she felt that she might go a little further.

She pushed herself up out of the water and sat on the edge of the bath. She sprayed a little of the shave gel into her hand, and rubbed it in her fingers. It started to foam up.

Jessica put her hand to her pussy and started to massage the gel into the hair there. It foamed and created a slick coating over her pussy. Jessica worked her hand through and around, and then let her middle finger gently slip between her lips.

She gasped as it rubbed up against the nub of her clitoris, causing a surge of pleasure through her body. She rubbed again and nearly dropped the razor in the bath.

Jessica smiled. Time for that a little later. She had heard that sex was a lot more pleasurable when the hair was removed ... the skin more sensitive to the touch.

Leaning forward, Jessica grasped the razor and took a breath. She had never done this before. And once done, it could not be undone. She would have to wait for the hair to regrow if she regretted the decision.

No regrets. She moved the razor and shaved off the area above her pussy. The skin was shiny and smooth as she cleared it of hair, and so she worked further down. Easing the blade through and across her pussy lips. She kept checking with her fingers, and re-shaved from different angles as she found areas she had missed.

With each stroke, more hair was removed, and her pussy was revealed. She had neat little lips framing her slit. Within was the soft pink flesh and the hooded nub of her clitoris above the sensitive walls leading to her vagina. She stopped and admired her handiwork. No hair remained at all. She was completely bald down there now.

Jessica sat back down in the hot bath and washed the remains of the soap away. The water seemed hotter somehow, and she was more aware of it on her nether regions. As she rubbed her hand against her pussy to remove the soap, she felt tremors of pleasure running through her body. She sighed and laid back.

Her hand continued to gently rub against her, and her fingers found their way between her lips, massaging her clitoris and brushing against her hole. She gasped and rubbed a little harder.

Even under the water she could feel her juices start to flow, and her fingers were slick against her skin. She dipped one finger lower and felt it enter her. A throb of pleasure hit her, and she noticed that her nipples had become erect in the bath. With her hand still playing down below, she let the other caress her breast and gently pinch her nipple. A shockwave of pleasure lanced from her nipple to her clitoris and back again. Jessica closed her eyes to the sensation and let her hand rub her harder. Harder. Faster.

With a gasp Jessica came, her legs bucking, and water splashing over the sides of the bath and onto the floor. She moaned with pleasure and gently rubbed her pussy as the orgasm quieted. Taking care of herself had never been that good before.

She smiled and thought that perhaps she would try staying bald for the moment … Could be interesting.

Jessica lay in the cooling water for around an hour, letting her mind drift back and forth from Leo to Marco, from the play to her mysterious new lover. She was happier than she had been for some time, and felt that maybe life was starting to get better for her.

Eventually, she pushed herself up out of the water and wrapped her hair in a towel. She dried her body with a second towel, rubbing the water away. She checked her pussy again, and nodded with satisfaction. She had done a good job. Completely smooth, with no stray hairs. Her fingers liked the feel of the skin there too. She slowly stroked again, imagining what her lover's fingers might now feel like. She smiled. Hopefully it wouldn't be too long.

Wrapped in her robe, Jessica went back into her room, and her eyes fell on her mobile phone. The screen was alight, which could only mean one thing. She pounced on it and checked it. There was a message.

'TONIGHT. 8PM. BALCONY. BE THERE.'

Jessica drew in a long breath as her legs turned to jelly and her stomach flip-flopped. She knew she would be there. And she would hopefully find out more about her strange benefactor.

6

The balcony was dark when Jessica arrived. She peered around the doorway in the half-light, trying to make out if anyone was waiting there. It seemed to be empty, so she made her way down through the seats to the front.

The stage below was in darkness. The deep red velvet curtains were pulled across and the area was lit only by a single emergency light that glowed from the side of the stage. This was always lit, allowing anyone to see their way even in the event of a power cut.

Jessica thought that the stage looked lonely and forlorn like this. Stages were meant to be used. To be performed upon, the ballet or play watched by an eager audience. To see it empty and desolate and quiet made her yearn to fill it herself with light and dance.

She looked around the balcony area again, half hoping that Marco would be there, emerging from the shadows to take her hand. There was no-one there. She checked her phone. The light from the screen illuminated her face. It was 19:58. She smiled. Perhaps her mysterious stranger played everything exactly by the clock.

Jessica sat in one of the seats and closed her eyes. It

was quiet and the place smelt slightly musty. She loved the smell of the theatre, the seats, the curtains, the enticing scents of greasepaint, sweat and hard work.

Dead on 20:00 there was a click behind her. The door opened and then closed gently. She opened her eyes and looked over toward the entrance. There was a shape there. A man. And clearly he was very reliable. Jessica liked that.

'Don't be afraid,' said the voice. Deep and reassuring. 'I'm glad you came.'

'I got your message,' said Jessica, a slight catch in her voice.

The man moved through the seats towards her. His head and face were in shadow, but Jessica could see his body. He was wearing a pair of dancers' sweatpants and a tight-fitting top that showed the lines of his muscles.

'We need to talk about dance,' he said. 'And about your taking the lead in the forthcoming production.'

Jessica shook her head. 'Leo and Rowan have the leads,' she said. 'I am just the understudy.'

The man stopped. 'There is no "just" about being the understudy,' he said with a note of reproach in his voice. 'The understudy is one of the most important roles there is. It is you who will take over when something … happens … to the lead.'

'What do you mean? Is something going to happen to Rowan?'

The man stopped moving forward and stood, his head still in darkness.

'Who knows what might occur?' he said gently.

Jessica took a breath. 'What do you want to do then?' she asked, still not sure of this man or what was happening.

'You are tense,' came the reply. 'We must start by

loosening you up a little, yes? Every good rehearsal must start with a warm-up.'

The man stepped forward again, and his head fell into the dim light. Jessica could see that his hair was slicked back with the shining oil that all the male dancers used, so that it was impossible to tell what his real hairstyle was like. But his face ... his face was covered by a mask.

Jessica gasped involuntarily. This was like something out of classical literature. The mask was black and covered the whole of the upper part of the man's face. Only his lips could be seen, pursed and waiting. His eyes were dark pits in the mask, glinting slightly in the dim light, but aside from that, there was nothing to suggest who this man might be. The mask was sculptured, and presented fine cheekbones. There were also suggestions of brows and nose in the mask as well, but nothing to give a hint of who might be behind it.

Jessica looked at the lips. She felt they might be familiar and tried to recall what Marco's lips were like ... but divorced from the rest of the features, she found this impossible.

'How ... how do you want to start then?' she stammered. She felt very much like a girl on a first date, but deep within her she wanted and yearned for this stranger to touch her again. To take her. She felt the first stirrings of lust as she spoke, and hoped that her eagerness was not heard in her voice.

'Turn around.' It was an instruction, not a request.

Jessica swallowed and turned again to face the stage, leaning her arms against the balustrade in the same way as she had done the previous day.

There was a gentle rustling as the man moved closer to her.

'Now.' His voice was close to her ear now, almost whispering. 'We must relieve you of your tensions and stresses, and then we can begin the class.'

She felt his hand touch her in the small of her back.

'I want you to stretch your legs out. One at a time, back and forth, though gently.'

Jessica tentatively stretched out one leg and tensed it.

'Good. Now the other.'

This was the one with the injured hip, so Jessica stretched it out, but stopped when the slight twinge of pain came.

'Good,' the stranger whispered. 'Now your arms. Above your head and stretch.'

Jessica stood and put her arms up. She reached for the sky and tensed and stretched them.

She felt two hands gently take her by the waist and rest there, supporting her.

'Now over your head, one, then the other.'

Jessica took one of her arms over her head and felt the muscles tense again as she stretched. Then she repeated with the other.

She relaxed back, dropping her arms to her sides. The hands remained on her waist.

'You are still tense,' came the voice, and Jessica felt she could hear a note of amusement in it. 'We need to relax you more. Place your hands behind your head.'

Jessica did as instructed, and felt the hands gently smooth from her waist around to her stomach, and up to her breasts. In this position, the material of her dance top was taut against them, and her nipples were prominent, partly from the coolness of the theatre but mostly from the excitement and her arousal. The hands cupped her breasts, and she gasped as the thumbs gently moved over her nipples, back and forth, stroking them and bringing them to further prominence.

She moved her hands and felt the side of the man's head. He dipped and placed a kiss on the nape of her neck.

Jessica shuddered gently as sparks of emotion flittered down her spine. His hands caressed her as he continued to plant light kisses on her neck again, trailing his wet tongue across the top of her backbone. Her hands touched his head as he moved, not pushing him away, but encouraging him.

He pulled back slightly, and she felt herself pushed back over the balcony. Her hands gripped the rail as she felt the back of her dance skirt lifted and her rump exposed to the air.

Her mind was aflame. She wanted him so badly. She wiggled her bottom gently as the hands caressed it, moaning gently as the fingers found the top of her panties, and she felt them eased down her legs. She lifted one foot and then the other to allow them to be removed.

She felt even more nervous this time. It passed through her mind that she didn't know who the man was, or anything about him. Mostly this excited her, but still there was a dark fear that crept into that instinctive part of her brain. He could be *anybody.* He could be capable of anything. Yet here she was turning her back on him and allowing him intimacies that she wouldn't even give to a boyfriend on their second date. Jessica pulled back from this thought. This wasn't a date, after all. It was a rendezvous. A secret and dangerous liaison that could lead to anything. But that was precisely why it excited her. She felt as though she had no control.

She felt cool air between her legs, and with a moment's shock realised that the man's head must be level with that area now – he had crouched to help remove her panties. She felt a gentle kiss placed on her left buttock, and then on her right.

Instinctively she shifted her balance, spreading her legs a little more because her hip ached.

Jessica closed her eyes as she felt fingers caressing up her thighs, gently stroking and touching and getting closer to her centre with every moment. Then there was an electric moment when she felt his clever touch over her shaven pussy. Soft fingertips exploring her there. She heard him take a sharp breath. It pleased and frightened her, because for a moment she wasn't sure exactly what this meant. Did he like what she had done, or was he disgusted by it?

'I see you have prepared,' came the voice. 'I like that.'

'I … I … Oh God,' was all Jessica could manage as a finger separated the folds of her lips and stroked inside, taking the moisture from her innermost parts and spreading it across her lips and over her clitoris.

'What do you want?' asked the voice. 'Tell me, and it shall be yours.'

'I … I want …' Jessica swallowed. Lust was making it hard for her to speak. 'I want … whatever you want to do to me.'

There. She had said it. It was out there. She was giving him *carte blanche* to do what he wanted, and the thought of it excited her so much that her pussy grew moist at his touch.

'So … what might be the best way to relax you?'

Jessica knew it was a rhetorical question. A thought he was speaking aloud. She shuddered as the man moved back from her momentarily, and she found herself concentrating on the stage curtains again.

Breathing deeply to take her mind away from the aching lust that warmed her pussy.

He spread her gently, and she felt the head of his large dick bobbing against her entrance. The sensation was incredible. Her shaved skin was electric. Every touch was sensitive, and as he pushed forward, his cock entered her smoothly, causing ripples of pleasure through her body, because she was ready for him.

Jessica gasped as he reached the limit of penetration. She could feel her inner muscles gripping his length. Could sense that the head of his cock was pushed up against her womb. She felt totally filled. A shudder rippled through her at the feeling of being pinned like that. She couldn't move, because he was tensed inside her, revelling in the sensation of filling her. He pulled back, and she felt momentary loss as the length was removed from her. But then it was back again, thrust in slowly.

As Jessica stood, legs splayed, leaning against and over the balcony, the man fucked her firmly. As he did so, Jessica felt the arousal and lust grow and build within her. She wanted to be taken harder. Faster. But he did not comply. She tried pushing back against him with more urgency, but he resisted and continued with the slow, comfortable screw that he was giving her. It was agonising and torturous. She wanted it hard but was afraid to say it.

His hands gripped her waist as he controlled the pace, urging her forward and backwards on his cock. Jessica bit her lip. She was still afraid to make any sound in case she was overheard. The passion rose within her, and with a jolt she came, just a small tremor, enough to make her tense her arms. The resultant liquid eased the passage of the cock a little, and it moved more slickly within her. It made his size easier to take and the orgasm she experienced only increased her excitement and need for more. This caused the friction to change, and in turn the cockhead rubbed gently against her g-spot as she was fucked. She started to shake her head a little as the passion rose again. She was moaning gently to herself, eyes closed, focusing on the sensation as this amazing stranger took her. She felt unable to stop him, even if she had wanted to.

He slowed his pace a little, teasing her with his movements. She moaned louder, and he resumed fucking her a little harder. The entire length of his magnificent cock powering into her body, his balls slapping gently against her arse on each inward stroke. Then, she was closer … the pleasure was mounting. She felt so desperate for total release and ready now to really let go.

Jessica realised that she was moaning loudly on each stroke, and recalled how Leo's conquests had done the same. It annoyed her a little, taking the edge off her lust, but she pushed it aside. *This is what I wanted. This is what I needed,* she told herself. She forced herself to focus in on the sensation and felt her orgasm building. The pressure coming … She gripped the rail harder and cried out as the stranger took her cue and fucked her faster, his cock slickly moving in and out of her soaking pussy.

Then she was there. Sparks exploded in her mind and body simultaneously as her orgasm hit, the biggest she had ever had. Her muscles convulsed and tried to grip the member that was so successfully pleasuring her, but the lubrication made this impossible, and instead the movement sent her into further spasms that prolonged the climax. As he moved so she came. Over and over she twitched with pleasure, bathing his cock with her juices as she came hard. She forgot what time it was, what day it was, who she was … All that mattered was the electric jolts running up and down her body, making her arms grip the rail and her legs turn to jelly, shuddering as the intense feelings pulsed through her body.

She gulped for air and shuddered. The man's movements slowed, allowing her to gently come down from her orgasmic high. He slowed and rested. His cock still enormous, plugging her pussy.

Jessica breathed in, releasing the air in a whoop. She shook her head, her ponytail whipping. She relaxed her grip and breathed in again.

The gentle hands released her, and the man stepped back, his cock emerging from her with a slurping noise. Jessica heard the rustle as he made himself decent once more.

'Shit,' she was surprised to hear herself use such a word. 'You're a bit good at that, aren't you?'

'And you,' came the response.

Jessica couldn't believe what she was hearing – she was not good … but she felt herself blush at the compliment.

'How are you feeling now?' asked the stranger.

Jessica thought for a moment. 'Relaxed,' she said.

'Good.'

The stranger stepped back again. 'Now, come with me to the studio, we have work to do.'

Jessica smiled and pushed herself up from the balcony. Her legs were still shaking, and her pussy was quivering and a little sore from the treatment it had just received, but she felt good. More than that, she felt fulfilled and satisfied. So this was what good sex made you feel like … No wonder people kept coming back for more.

She retrieved her panties from the floor, smiling at the comparison she made between herself and Leo's girls, and followed the man as he made his way to the door of the balcony. He led her quickly through the corridors and to one of the studios on the upper floor of the Acadamie. One that was not used very often, as the lighting needed work and the mirrors that lined one wall were a little tarnished and desilvered.

She watched the man closely, looking for any sign that she might know who he was. He was well-built and athletic. Dressed in a pair of dance sweats and a tight top; but then everyone wore those. On his feet were a pair of simple plimsolls, so no clues there either.

His face was hidden by the mask, which she could now see was not black but a deep blue, with tracings of silver around the eyes and nose. It covered everything and there was no way she could make out who he was. There was a slight ridge over the eyes of the mask that cast shadow on his eyes. She tried to make out their colour but it was impossible in this light. They could have been brown or blue and she would never be sure.

Jessica sighed. It looked like she was going to have to live in the dark about her mystery lover for the moment.

The man turned back to face her.

'Now, Jessica, it's time to start on the dance,' he said, keeping his voice low.

He was holding the book for *Appollon Musagete* in his hand.

'Act one. Scene one.'

Jessica smiled, and moved into position for the start of the play. As long as she took things easy, her hip did not bother her. And the more exercise she got, the stronger it felt, and the more confident she became in performing. This stranger seemed determined to help her – and in more ways than one – and, given her standing in the Acadamie at the moment, this could be no bad thing.

7

'Anthony!'

Jessica smiled as she hurried across the hallway to where Anthony was waiting.

'Hi Jessica,' he grinned. 'How's it going?'

Jessica reached him and gestured to his leg. 'How's your leg doing?'

'Not too bad today,' he said. 'And I notice that yours seems better as well.'

Jessica nodded. 'I've been doing some gentle exercise each day, just as the doctor told me. I'm a good girl,' she preened.

If only Anthony knew just how good a girl I've been, she thought. *Apparently I'm a very good girl indeed.*

'That's good,' said Anthony, breaking her chain of thought. 'I've not heard anything more about the Acadamie though. It does seem as though they are pinning their hopes on this play.'

Jessica smiled. 'I need to talk to you about something,' she said.

Returning to her room after the training with the masked

man the previous night, Jessica had felt exhausted and fulfilled all at the same time.

The dance instruction had been nothing short of brilliant. The man had known exactly what moves would work, and at what point in order to bring out the story and emphasise the dance that told it. He had also been sympathetic to her injury, concentrating on arm and body movements rather than the more complex and energetic leg work, but even so, she had felt like she was flying through the air on more than one occasion.

When they had finished around an hour of training, she had turned around and found he was nowhere to be seen. It was like he had vanished into the air as silently as he had arrived. Jessica had picked up her belongings and made her way back to her own room, lost in her own thoughts, with her muscles aching gently from the workout.

Her pussy was aching too, the sensitive skin remembering the touch and feeling of being loved so comprehensively. Jessica adored the feeling, and threw herself back on her bed with a happy smile on her face. Her only regret was that the stranger hadn't come inside her again. It seemed he had been more concerned about relaxing her than taking his own pleasure. She wasn't sure what to think of this but took it as a positive sign. He wasn't, she hoped, going to turn out like Leo.

She stripped off her sweaty dance top and damp panties and took a long, hot shower. Just the job to ease her limbs and to sluice away all of the perspiration. She undid her ponytail and washed her long dark hair as well. Soaping it up until it squeaked in her fingers, then conditioning it to make it shine.

She stood and looked at herself in the mirror and could see the inner glow of confidence in her face and eyes. This made her happy, even though the realisation that it was all down to someone she didn't even know still rang an alarm bell. She felt beautiful and attractive and it showed on her relaxed features.

Jessica sat on her bed and thought it through.

The man had to be someone in the Acadamie. It just wasn't possible for a complete stranger to get into and out of the place like that. Moreover he knew the layout and how to get from room to room. He also knew what dance was being rehearsed, and she was sure she had never told him that.

So who was he? She still felt it might be Marco, and deep inside her she hoped it was. It certainly wasn't Leo. He had been on the stage the first time the stranger had come to her. And she had seen how he went about his sexual conquests. There was little passion in Leo, just taking. This was completely different from how she felt about her stranger. His passion had been real somehow, in tune with her. Knowing what she wanted and giving it to her without her having to voice it herself. Or at least she hoped that was the case.

But there was also danger here. If she didn't know who this person was, then what if he hurt her? It was obvious to her that there was a degree of obsession there, and that sort of lust could easily tip over into violence if she wasn't careful. But what could she do? She had heard about women who had fallen into abusive relationships, led to believe that the man loved them. This was different though, wasn't it?

Jessica mulled over in her mind, and realised that she wanted to keep seeing the man. She liked the sex. Fuck, that was an understatement. She *loved* the sex, and she also enjoyed the dance tuition. The stranger knew what he was doing, and she felt that if she persisted then she would get better and better. Deep down she was afraid she was being used though. What was his motive after all? Why was he helping her? Surely it wasn't just because he wanted her?

So she would have to try and protect herself.

That was when she thought of Anthony.

He had confided in her on more than one occasion, and so far at least she had managed to keep all his secrets.

Perhaps she could trust him with this secret of her own? The more she thought about it, the more she realised that was the answer. To let Anthony know what was happening, so that if anything untoward occurred, then he could be her back-up.

She finished drying herself off and slipped into her pyjamas, noting that they were soft and comfy against her skin. She would talk to Anthony the next day, and see what he thought. That was the best bet.

Anthony raised one eyebrow and leaned on his stick.

'Special tuition?' he asked.

Jessica nodded. 'He's training me to dance *Appollon Musagete.*'

Anthony smiled. 'But that's not all ...'

Jessica blushed and she knew it. She grinned, and that was all Anthony needed to see. He grinned back at her.

'Well ... I guess I can keep an eye out. So, you'll let me know where and when you're meeting this chap, so that I'll know where you were should anything happen?'

Jessica nodded. 'Yes. That's about it.'

Anthony shook his head. 'Things I do for you ...' he muttered.

'Oh thank you!' Jessica gave him a big hug. 'This means a lot to me,' she said.

'I can see. And I can see that you have a glow about you,' he noted. 'Something is good for you anyway, and that can only help. I won't ask if he's any good in bed ...'

8

'Watch where you're going!'

Natalie pushed past Jessica roughly in the corridor. As usual her retinue tittered and followed on behind her.

How old do they think they are? wondered Jessica as she watched them go. They were acting like high school brats off some television show rather than mature women learning to dance the classics.

She shifted her folder to the other arm and continued on back to her room.

Over the last week, the pain in her hip had declined, and clearly the lessons and gentle exercise she had been taking were helping. She smiled to herself. Her mysterious benefactor had been summoning her every other evening for special tuition, and although her limbs always ached afterwards, she really looked forward to their sessions. The next should be that night, and in preparation, Jessica had been working her arms and upper body during the day as she had been asked. She would have to lift the male lead momentarily in *Appollon Musagete,* and needed strength in her arms to be able to achieve that. Of course no dance would require the female lead actually to have to exert to lift the male – it was all part of a complex sequence of moves that had been worked out for the climax, where the male jumped up and over the female, spinning in the air as he did so. The female then had to provide a small push in mid-air to allow the male to complete the jump and land back on his feet on the other side. Visually impressive stuff, but actually quite simple to execute: as long as the male didn't crush the female on the way over.

As she passed the main hall, Jessica paused and looked in. A group of the boys were practicing, and Jessica's eye was caught by Marco. He was dressed in a pair of shorts and a T-shirt and she could see the muscles rippling in his legs and arms as he moved. She stood by the door watching him. The group started with a *plié* and then moved across the floor in unison.

Jessica thought that Marco was probably the most graceful of them all, and she saw that he had his eyes closed as he danced. She often did that as well. It was easier to lose yourself in the movement that way.

As he reached the end of the movement, he opened his eyes and looked straight at her. Jessica swallowed and smiled, feeling the blush bloom on her cheeks. She pushed herself away from the door and continued her on her way. Sure, it couldn't hurt for him to have seen her watching. At least that's what she told herself.

She pushed open the door to her room and threw her folder on the bed. First things first, and after the day's work, she wanted a shower.

She set the shower running in the bathroom and stripped off her clothes, again admiring herself in the mirror. Her arms were starting to look more toned already, and the bruise on her leg was starting to fade. Not bad.

Entering the shower she gasped as the hot needles

of water hit her. *Nothing like a good hot shower*, she thought. She soaped over her body, washing away the day's sweat and grime. She picked up her razor and, resoaping herself, carefully reshaved her pubic mons and pussy. They were starting to feel a little stubbly, and she wanted herself to be perfect for that night's escapade.

Of course it wasn't just the dance sessions that got her blood boiling and her heart racing, but the sex too. Never before had she made love in so many different ways and positions, and certainly not in the public and semi-public places that her lover chose for them. It was all exciting, and she couldn't wait to find out what he had planned for her that night.

She left the shower and dried off with a towel, humming the music to the dance to herself. It had a nice tune and rhythm, and although she had been going over the moves during the day with the rest of the selected cast, she couldn't help but feel Rowan's eyes boring into her back all the time. She was deliberately favouring her hip more than necessary during the day classes as well. For some reason she didn't want the rest of them to see that she was healing faster than perhaps they expected. And she certainly didn't want them to arrange another little accident for her as a result. So it was better to let them think that she was hurt and hurting, and then they might leave her alone.

The text arrived, almost like clockwork, at 7 pm. She loved how reliable he was; she didn't have to worry and stress herself over not hearing from him. It was something she expected all of Leo's girls did, and she was grateful that he had never turned his attention to her.

Jessica had showered and dried herself and was seated on her bed, idly combing her long hair. That night she felt she wanted to eschew her usual tight bun and leave her hair loose. She had an emergency scrunchie in her bag and, like all the girls, carried hairpins all the time. You never knew when a stray hair might fall and get in the way.

It was then that her phone vibrated and pinged and she snatched it up eagerly.

'ROOM 705. 7.30 PM' read the text.

Jessica smiled and carried on brushing her hair out. She had time to let Anthony know where she would be and when, get her hair sorted, and get changed before her assignation.

Room 705 was one of the unused dance rooms on the top floor of the Acadamie. It was interesting how her benefactor liked to use the out-of-the-way rooms … almost as though he knew the layout of the place intimately. This meant that he had to be someone who was there with her every day.

As she made her way to the room, Jessica wondered again who he might be … Marco was still her number one choice, but there were several others. Peter perhaps. He always seemed to spend more time watching her than concentrating on the lessons. Or maybe Carlos. Carlos had the nicest smile she had ever seen, but like most of the boys, he didn't seem to know that she existed.

The door to room 705 was unlocked, and she pushed it open and went in. Inside it was gloomy, the place lit by a single candle placed on the floor. Alongside it was a *chaise longue* and on the chair was the stranger. He was watching her as she entered the room, and smoothly rose and offered her his hand as she approached.

'Jessica,' he said, and as always his hushed voice raised the hairs on the back of her neck. 'Thank you for being so punctual.'

'That's fine,' she replied. And then with a smile: 'It's not like there's much else to do around here.'

The man nodded his assent, and went to the door. Jessica heard a key click in the lock, and a moment of panic blossomed in her chest.

'Just so that we're not interrupted,' said the man, smiling.

Jessica could see his mouth below the mask. A small smile played over his lips. It was soft and kind, not cynical in the way that Leo smiled. She knew that he wouldn't hurt her.

'What tonight, then?' she asked, spinning on the spot and making the candle flicker.

'Tonight? Well, tonight is your pleasure,' he said, stepping closer to her.

Jessica gasped gently. What did he mean? Her pleasure?

He took her hand and softly brought it to his lips, kissing it.

'I mean,' he said in a whisper, 'that tonight you will be pleasured.'

Jessica looked at him, eyes wide. All manner of things were running through her head at that moment, and most of them were stimulating.

The stranger moved towards her and took her hand again, then pulled on her fingers so that she was standing with her back to him, his arms wrapped around her and her arms held in his. He dipped his head and gently kissed the back of her neck.

The hairs there stood up and a shudder went through her body.

'What's wrong?' he asked, feeling her tremble.

'Nothing,' Jessica said. 'Just anticipation.'

'And you like anticipation, don't you?'

Jessica paused for a moment and then nodded.

'Anticipation can lead to great things. But to really fulfil them – I mean *really* fulfil them – you have to learn how to let yourself go.'

Jessica frowned. 'Let myself go …? But …?'

'I have been watching you, Jessica. Observing you. And I have noted that you have a reserve. A part of you holds back. You are afraid of failure perhaps, or of someone seeing you as a fool?'

'No … I … I …'

'But this is hindering your dancing. To truly dance, to truly believe, you have to let go. You have to not care if you fail – for in not caring, you will truly succeed. Besides, you could learn so much from taking risks. You've played it safe for too long.'

The man led Jessica closer to the *chaise longue* and gently released her, pushing her to sit there. She did so, upright at first and then leaning back as he moved towards her. She could smell some sort of scent on him. A musk that merged with his own scent, creating a unique aroma that intoxicated her. His breath was slightly minty as he leaned forward and kissed her on the lips.

'And so, Jessica,' he said. 'Tonight's lesson will be about letting go. No-one can hear you here. No-one is watching you. No-one is judging you. So you can escape. You can let your mind and body free. And learn what it is to let go completely.'

Jessica nodded, and the man pushed her back against the *chaise longue* so that her back was supported on the raised end and one leg was resting against the padded material of the couch. The other leg was on the floor.

The stranger turned his back to her, and Jessica wondered what he was doing, but then he removed his top, baring his muscled and defined chest. She looked appreciatively at him. Not much hair, nice taut skin … certainly very nice to look at. He was masked yet naked. It excited her more than she could believe to finally see any of his body. She wondered if he was planning to finally reveal his identity, but the mask stayed implacably on his face. She looked up into his eyes, which were, as usual, dark pools. The candlelight glinted off the planes of the mask and made the silver inlay twinkle and sparkle.

He kneeled beside the *chaise*. One hand stroked Jessica's face while the other moved down her neck, fingers tracing a line over her breast bone. She felt a shudder as her body responded to him.

His hands fell down to her thighs and she felt them move up under her chemise and to her panties. *Why did I actually bother to put any on?*, she thought with a smile, and lifted her bottom to allow him to slide them down and off her legs.

She settled back into the couch as he stroked down her legs to her feet and eased off the ballet shoes she had been wearing. Her toes were usually confined, so now she stretched them out, enjoying the freedom of not being in a pair of *pointe* shoes or even ballet slippers.

She closed her eyes for a moment in pleasure as she felt her feet being massaged by strong hands. The thumbs easing up the underside of her feet, and then the fingers massaging each of her toes in turn. It was relaxing and sensual. Jessica felt totally comfortable with him, despite all of the misgivings she'd had in the first few weeks.

The hands moved up from her feet to her calves, massaging and moving and caressing as they went. Jessica felt amazing, as though her legs were being touched by angels. There was such tenderness in every caress. Despite his brusque way of speaking to her, Jessica always felt he treated her with care and affection. He began planting kisses on her legs too, just behind where his hands were moving. And they were moving upwards still, over her knees and to her thighs.

As the kisses reached her inner thighs, she moaned gently, stretching herself on the couch and moving her legs further apart to allow him access.

'That's good,' he murmured between kisses. 'Show your appreciation. I like that.'

Jessica put her hands on the man's head as he kissed farther upwards. His hands were now stroking her mons, thumbs moving gently in circles as his head dipped to kiss and caress her thighs. He was so close now to her pussy that she felt intense anticipation of what he might do next.

When she felt that she couldn't take it any longer, his head moved slightly, and a wet tongue moved over her pussy lips, dampening them and making her shudder with delight.

She sighed, opening her legs wider to encourage him.

He shifted position slightly, bending her knees and spreading her legs farther apart, as he knelt before her, head between her legs and hands and arms stroking her stomach and pubic area.

He looked up at her, face implacable behind the mask, eyes glittering and with a faint smile on his mouth. 'Shall we begin?'

Without waiting for an answer, he dipped his head, and Jessica felt a gentle kiss at the top of her pussy, immediately followed by his tongue burrowing down between her lips and gently teasing her. Unlike before, however, the teasing continued, and she moaned as his clever tongue twitched and moved and caressed the folds of sensitive skin over and around her clitoris.

Jessica pushed back into the couch, her arms and hands fluttering a little as the sensations washed over her. She felt the involuntary rock of her hips as he licked her. She couldn't believe what she was feeling. It was as though someone had connected an electric cable directly from the pleasure centres of her brain straight to her cunt. And that there were additional feeds going to her breasts and nipples, which were erect and sensitive under the dance top.

She rested her hands on the man's head, stroking his slicked-back hair gently, as his lips and tongue played with her pussy.

The tongue would lap around her clit, and then he would push closer, allowing him to lap lower, the organ brushing over and around her entrance, making her pulse with pleasure. As he worked her, so the feelings grew and grew. She started to twitch gently as the tongue circled her clit and flicked repeatedly over and around it.

He was speeding up as well; a part of her brain realised this as his tongue moved faster over her, teasing her and raising her to another level. She felt a spasm deep inside her, and her legs shuddered as a small orgasm went through her.

The stranger lifted his head and smiled at her again. 'You're getting wet,' he commented, and then dipped his head again to continue feasting on her.

She moaned more loudly and her head started to shake from side to side, not in denial of what was happening, but in acceptance. She felt his hands slide over her stomach, gently caressing her there. His thumbs moving down to her mons and rubbing against the smooth skin. His arms were locked around her legs, holding her to his mouth, so no matter how she tried to squirm, his tongue and lips were locked onto her most sensitive area, and he was bringing her closer and closer and closer …

'Ohhhhh God!' she moaned, thrashing her head as another climax ripped through her body. This was stronger than the last, and made her fingers clench involuntarily against his head. She moved them as she was worried about hurting him, and dug them into the velvet covering on the couch.

She closed her eyes tight and concentrated on what he was doing – that intensified the feelings and she came again, loving what he was doing to her. She squirmed then, pulling back because now she was so sensitive she couldn't take anymore.

The stranger slowed his movements again, and lifted his mouth from her. She looked down and could see her juices glistening on his lips. She felt incomplete somehow and wished that he would now finish her off.

'Remember what I said, Jessica. You have to learn how to let go …'

She smiled and nodded. Her breath coming in gasps, her heart beating hard.

She gasped again as she felt one of his fingers

gently probe her, touching the entrance to her, and sliding around and in and around …

'That's a good girl,' the man whispered. 'Now then …'

He dipped his head again, and Jessica felt the most incredible sensations as his tongue lapped at her sensitive clitoris, while at the same time his finger gently stroked and penetrated her. She thrashed her head from side to side, the tension in her body mounting once more. She had already cum twice, and could now feel the mother of all orgasms building in her body. She was an instrument, and this stranger was playing her perfectly, anticipating her needs, touching, stroking, licking … bringing her higher and higher.

'Christ … I … *Omigod!* … Shit …' she wasn't even sure what she was saying any more. The pleasure was coming fast and strong, and her legs were shuddering and shaking as he continued to lick and touch her.

Faster and faster. He ran his tongue around and around.

Jessica felt her body crest and pulse with pleasure and she lost control.

She screamed out loud as her entire body convulsed, and shards of pleasure shot from her clitoris and pussy throughout her body. Her hands spasmed and clutched helplessly at the velvet as she came so strongly that all thought was excised from her mind. She gasped and panted as she came again, more strongly still, and the tendons in her neck stood out as she shuddered, her whole body orgasming in one glorious release of energy as it exploded with pleasure.

Electricity pulsed through Jessica and her eyes were full of sparks and stars as her brain processed the pleasure she was receiving.

The stranger slowed his movements as she came, keeping her in a state of extreme pleasure by licking her very tenderly. He removed his finger from her now-oversensitive pussy, and let her ride the wave of pleasure back down again.

Her shuddering decreased, and the man gently stroked her thighs as her breathing started to return to normal. Her hands relaxed and her body fell back against the couch. Her now-hypersensitive pussy was engorged with blood, and was puffy and soaking wet against his tongue. He kissed her one last time then pulled away.

Jessica returned to Earth slowly. She didn't know what day it was. Who she was. Where she was. All she knew was the pleasure and sensation she had given herself over to. It ebbed and flowed in her veins still, and she opened her eyes, momentarily puzzled by the lights and what she could see. Her eyes returned to focus on the man kneeling between her thighs. One hand stroking her leg, a mask on his upper face, and a gentle smile on his lips.

Jessica blinked and smiled back. Could she even speak? She could feel her heart thumping in her chest still, and the remnants of the delight she had experienced, flitting around in the back of her brain. She realised that this was exactly what was meant by 'having your brains fucked out,' and hot on the heels of that thought was that she had never, ever, ever experienced anything like that before.

She forced her face into a smile.

'Wow.'

'It's okay,' said the man, 'I know it's hard to think.'

'You're not kidding,' said Jessica. 'Sheesh. I've never had … I mean … that's the most amazing … Hell

… How do you *do* that?'

The stranger smiled again and gracefully stood. He held out his hand to her and helped her into a seated position on the *chaise longue*.

'Well I can't go giving away all my secrets,' he said.

'Whew … Well that's a secret I guess people would pay good money to know!'

'How are you feeling?'

Jessica drew in a deep breath and released it. 'Good. It's amazing what a good orgasm can do.'

'And how did you feel about losing control?'

Jessica looked at the man. 'It was … good,' she said, staring into his eyes and trying to divine what he might be thinking. 'I felt alive and thrilled to be able to.'

'That's good. You must remember that feeling. It's the same as performing. You need to be able to relax and go for gold every time.'

'Well I'm certainly relaxed now.'

The man nodded. 'And that is also good. How do you feel about trying some of those trickier dance moves now?'

Jessica smiled. 'You are determined to get me dancing, aren't you?'

'You are beautiful when you dance,' said the man. 'You have outer beauty too, but when you dance, your inner beauty comes to the fore and you set the stage on fire.'

Jessica blushed at the compliment. 'Okay then, let's do it.' She paused for a moment, then added, 'And let's practice dancing as well.'

She grinned cheekily at the stranger, and he smiled back. 'I can see that things are improving for you, Jessica,' he said.

Jessica felt a warm glow inside her. Things certainly were improving. She felt amazing. Her hip wasn't even hurting anymore, and this man had brought her to the knowledge of her own body. Her lusts and desires. She had had no idea that she could enjoy sex so much. The only doubt that still remained was his persistence in always pleasing and pleasuring her. Jessica still couldn't understand what he ultimately gained from their contact, as he hadn't let himself go since the first night on the balcony.

Jessica took up her dance position and followed his instructions as always. That night she danced better than usual, and it was only partly to do with the orgasms he had given her. Another part of her was plotting and planning. She wanted to return the compliment. She wanted to give him back some of the pleasure he had been giving her. But how was that to happen? She really didn't know, since the stranger called all of the shots in both their sex and their dance practice.

9

The dinner lady dumped a turd of mashed potato onto Jessica's tray and handed it back to her.

Would it hurt her to smile? Jessica wondered as she said 'Thank you,' and took possession of the tray once more.

Dinnertime was always something of a chore for Jessica, mainly because she had few friends, and depending on what time the lessons and classes ended she could end up having no-one to sit with to eat. Eating alone was all very well, but it did become something of a trial when it happened too often.

She looked at her tray: a breast of chicken in some glutinous white sauce, a splodge of mash and a handful of peas. *I suppose it could be worse.*

She filled a paper cup with coke from the soda fountain and turned to see if there was anywhere to sit. Typical. Most of the place was already filled with students talking and eating. Arms gesticulating. There were even a couple of girls practicing their *pointe* over by the windows. Dance training never stopped.

Before heading off to find somewhere to sit, Jessica

did a quick scan for any of the usual suspects who might make her lunch even more unpleasant. She spotted Natalie over by the toilet doors. She was sitting with her usual group of followers and they were shrieking with laughter over some joke or person.

Jessica headed in the other direction, and found a seat near the corner. The table was occupied by a couple of boys from the class below her that she didn't know, so she thought it would be okay to sit there. The boys glanced at her but made no comment and resumed talking together.

She looked around. Peter and Carlos were seated over at another table. Peter glanced at her, and Jessica averted her eyes, studying her food.

She sneaked another look at him after a moment. He was wearing a bandana around his head, keeping his hair out of his eyes. Jessica liked that; it was something that not many of the boys thought to do, and their haircuts varied from short crew-cuts to long hair held in ponytails like the girls.

Jessica cut and munched her chicken. It was tasteless, but at least the sauce gave it a little moisture. She looked out at the canteen, at all the students going about their everyday lives. Not a single one of them had any idea that she was seeing someone … more than that, sleeping with him … fucking him … and that he was also tutoring her expertly in dance and technique and style. The masked man knew his stuff both sexually and professionally, and not for the first time Jessica wondered who he really was.

Someone passed by the table and popped a flier down in front of Jessica. She smiled a thank you and studied the leaflet. There was to be a social evening the following day, in the main ballroom, and all students were invited. Free drinks.

Now those were the words that she and every other student wanted to see. Free drinks. She had no real interest in socialising, but it would be good to get out of her room and away from her studies for an evening at least. She was not seeing her lover that night – she had a session organised for later – so it all fitted in perfectly.

The two boys picked up their trays and left the table. Jessica was alone for the moment. She continued eating in silence, thinking over how things were going.

There was a flurry of movement and two more students sat at her table. She looked up and recognised Yvette. Her long hair was slightly in disarray, and Jessica could see that she had been crying. Her friend seated alongside her leaned close and pushed a stray hair back over her ear.

'Tell me what happened?' the friend said. 'From the beginning.'

Yvette sniffed and rubbed her nose with the back of her hand.

'It's Leo,' she said.

Jessica started, and immediately composed herself. She looked again at the leaflet, studying it closely, pretending that she was not listening to the girls' conversation at all. She picked up her coke and sipped it, placing an expression of total indifference on her face.

'It's always Leo,' said the other girl, who Jessica did not recognise. 'What's he done this time?'

'Fucking scumbag,' sniffed Yvette. 'If I see him around then he won't dance for a month!'

She sipped the coke that the other girl had brought to the table.

'So … what happened?' the girl asked again.

'Well … you know that Leo is seeing Rowan? Well,

a few weeks back, I bumped into him in the corridor. He told me that everything was going wrong with Rowan and that he was feeling down, you know? So I was like, sympathetic, yeah? And well anyway, next time we saw each other, he's all touchy feely, stroking my arm and stuff, and saying that he finds me really fascinating and he wants to get to know me better.'

Jessica could see the other girl nodding out of the corner of her eye. And Yvette sipped some more coke before continuing.

'So, anyway, we went off for coffee, and Leo, he was so nice and polite. Interested in me and what I was doing.'

Interested in something, that's for sure, thought Jessica. She put down the leaflet and pretended to be absorbed in her mobile phone.

'So he walked me back to my room, and tried nothing on. Not even a kiss, you know? He was like a perfect gentleman. So next day, he texts me, says he had a lovely time and could we meet again. This time for a bite to eat maybe. So I text back yes.'

'So did you go?' asked the other girl.

Yvette nodded. 'Sure did. And this time … well … let's say that Leo had more to eat than just the pasta.'

Yvette managed a smile, and the other girl looked shocked. 'You mean you … and Leo …?'

'Yup. Three times that night.'

'Three?'

'Yes.' Yvette leaned in conspiratorially. 'Leo is a really good fuck! He's so big!'

The other girl's eyes widened. From her reaction, Jessica suspected that she hadn't yet been hit on by Leo, and furthermore, that when her time eventually came, she would be a happy and willing participant.

'So what happened?'

Yvette looked off into the distance. 'It was amazing,' she said with a dreamy lilt to her voice. 'I'd never cum so much …'

The other girl laughed. 'I mean. What happened with Leo? I don't want to hear all about your sordid secrets.'

'Thanks for cheering me up, Anna,' said Yvette. 'I really appreciate it.'

'Pleasure. Now tell me what that git did.'

'Well, after that, I sort of assumed that I was Leo's girl, you know? I didn't see much of him around, but I got texts, and we seemed to be cool. But then I saw him with Rowan, and they were like all over each other, so I had no idea what was going on. I was afraid to ask him as well, in case, you know, he thought I was being creepy or something. But then he texted me that he had been asked to advise on the casting for a new production … and if I was interested, I should meet him later on that evening.'

'A casting for what?'

'Well that's just it, I never found out. Turned out that he wanted to meet me for some fun …'

'Fun?'

'You know,' said Yvette, and mimed pushing something in her mouth as her tongue bulged her cheek from the inside. 'Fun …'

The other girl giggled and nodded.

'So anyway, after that, he went off, and I heard nothing more. Next he's blanking me in the corridor. And I saw him with Rowan again, lovey as you like, as though nothing had happened.'

'So what happened?'

'I fucking confronted him, didn't I. Big mistake. He

was all, like, not knowing what I was talking about. It was just a bit of fun … all that crap.'

Anna shrugged and toyed with the coke. 'Sounds like a bit of a put down to me.'

'Too right,' said Yvette. 'I feel such an idiot. He led me on.'

He does that to everyone, thought Jessica, though one part of her did have some sympathy for Yvette. *On the other hand,* she thought, *you didn't seem to be too resistant to sucking his cock when you thought he could help you.*

'He's a bastard,' said Anna. 'I bet he does that to a lot of girls.'

Yvette nodded, sniffing again. 'I guess I'll get over it,' she said.

Anna smiled. 'Atta girl,' she said. 'There's plenty more out there who won't treat you like shit too.'

Jessica started to put her dinner things together on the tray, popping her phone back in her pocket and continuing to feign complete indifference to the conversation at the other end of the table.

'Even so,' said Anna thoughtfully, 'at least you got to experience a really big cock!'

The girls giggled together and Jessica sighed inwardly. What was the betting that Anna would be enjoying the dubious delights of Leo on a future evening … secure in the knowledge that there was no way he would cheat on her, and that of course he was leaving Rowan, and so on, and so on.

For the moment, though, Yvette had been discarded it seemed. Jessica was surprised, because Leo liked a nice tight body and Yvette had that in spades. Oh well. Leo's loss as usual. But what on earth had to happen to put a stop to his escapades! He seemed untouchable.

Jessica stood, took her tray to the disposal conveyor and made her way out of the canteen. As she passed Natalie's table, the girls there suddenly went silent, and as she reached the door, she heard them all burst into laughter. Jessica looked back and caught Natalie's eye. It was obvious that they had just made some comment or joke about her ... Well, let them. Jessica determined to go to the social and stand her ground. She refused to be bullied into staying in her room.

She swept from the room and the door closed behind her. She would show them. In the meantime, she had another night with her lover to look forward to ...

10

The music was playing full blast when Jessica arrived at the social.

She had decided to get there a little after the start – she was fed up with turning up at events and functions on time, only to find that she was effectively then on her own for the first hour or so. So she made her way down a fashionable hour late, and pushed open the door.

The event was going well and the room was packed. There were students and teachers there from every year, and a DJ in the corner was playing a succession of popular numbers.

Jessica was always amazed that all these people, who worked, lived, breathed, danced, performed and studied the classical works of musical maestros long-dead would prefer to listen to some badly-written, repetitive, poorly sung and derivative pop music rather than some uplifting Vivaldi or Strauss. She shrugged. Okay, she liked the classical music too, but sometimes a bit of Girls Aloud or Take That allowed the brain to rest, and in doing so, to appreciate just a little bit more the works that informed their lives.

Jessica made her way over to the bar area and got

an orange juice. Although this was a social, it was organised by the Acadamie and so, typically, there was no alcohol allowed. It was free though, as promised. She stepped over to the side and spotted Anthony leaning against one of the tables. She moved over to him and smiled.

'Cheers!'

They touched their plastic glasses together and drank.

'How's things?' asked Anthony.

'Good. Good.'

'Have you seen what Leo and co are up to?' he asked, gesturing over the other side of the room.

There, Jessica could see Leo, Rowan and a couple of others seated at a table. All seemed to be normal, but then Leo lifted something wrapped in brown paper to the table and poured it into his glass.

Jessica smiled. So they had brought their own.

'Why didn't we think of that?' she asked.

'We did,' smiled Anthony, and showed Jessica a silver hip flask that he had in his hand.

Jessica looked at it, and then at Anthony, and they both burst into laughter.

'Let's find somewhere to sit,' she said, and headed off to the opposite side of the room from Leo. She didn't want her evening to be spoiled by having to look at his smug face all the time.

They found a couple of spaces on the end of a couch, and Jessica allowed Anthony to sit first. She held his stick as he sank into the soft material.

'Thanks.'

She settled down beside him. 'Leg no better then?'

'It comes and goes,' Anthony said. 'It's actually not too bad at the moment.'

Jessica nodded, letting her gaze rove over the assembled people in the room.

'So, how's it going with your mystery man?' asked Anthony. 'You saw him last night, didn't you?'

Jessica smiled. 'I sure did.'

'Well?' asked Anthony again, poking Jessica gently in the ribs. 'Spill the beans.'

'It's all going fine,' she said. 'The tuition is good, it's stretching me.'

Bent over on all fours as his big, hard cock stretched the walls of my pussy as it pumped into me.

'That's good,' said Anthony. 'But I do worry about you. These mysterious assignations with someone you don't even know. He's not done anything to hurt you, has he?'

'No,' confirmed Jessica. 'Nothing like that at all.' *Screaming in pleasure as he fucks me within an inch of my life.* 'He's a gentleman, very … attentive.' *Attentive to my breasts as he sucks my nipples hard, bringing them to tight peaks while his clever fingers probe and massage my pussy.*

'Well … You know if he does try any funny business, then you're to let me know. I don't want you to get hurt.'

Jessica turned her eyes to Anthony. He was so sweet, wanting the best for her.

'Last night,' she said, flicking her eyes back and forth to make sure that no-one was listening, 'he took me on my back, my legs up around my ears. It was shameless!'

Anthony's eyes widened.

'Yes, shameless. I was lying such that I couldn't make a move to stop him – not that I did want to stop him of course – and he took me.'

Anthony nodded and grinned at her. He was

looking a little uncomfortable.

'Oh. My. God. Anthony. You're not a woman so you wouldn't know ... but the feeling of being penetrated by a big, hard ...'

Anthony cleared his throat. 'Well. Yes. Of course. Well.'

Jessica giggled. 'Oh, you know I'm only teasing you. Thanks again for having my back on this.'

Anthony nodded, and changed the subject. 'How's the hip?'

'Much better, thanks. It's barely hurting me at all now. I think all the rest from the energetic dance moves, plus all the evening training is really working.'

Anthony seemed distracted.

'What's wrong?' asked Jessica.

'Nothing.'

'Well there must be something ... Maybe I shouldn't tell you all my little escapades?'

'It's fine,' Anthony looked a little pained. 'It's up to you what you get up to. I just want you to be safe.'

Jessica looked at him. She could sense that her talking about sex with this stranger was painful for him, and she wondered if he was holding a candle for her himself. He was a strange type himself, walking with the stick due to his own injury, invisible to everyone around the Acadamie. She liked Anthony, certainly, but he was best friend material, not lover.

She sighed. Why did relationships have to get so complicated all the time? Why couldn't people just be friends?

'It's okay,' she said, putting her hand on his arm. 'I know it's hard for you, but I really am so grateful that I have you to talk to about everything.' She gestured around. 'There's no-one else.'

'Not even Marco?' asked Anthony, nodding with his head.

Jessica's own eyes widened. 'Marco is here?'

'Yes. Just over there. Don't make it too obvious.'

Jessica shifted her position and glanced over to where Anthony had indicated. Marco was indeed there, leaning against a table, and watching her intently.

Jessica felt a blush starting up, so sipped her drink to try to hide it. She still had a deep suspicion that Marco was her masked stranger. At that moment, Leo swaggered past. He was wearing a pair of tight black trousers that clung to the contours of his bottom. His shirt was open to the stomach, and around his neck he had a gold chain. *Prat*, thought Jessica.

Hanging onto his arm was Rowan, dressed – if that was the right word – in a loose but clingy pants suit that emphasised her own very dramatic curves, and around them both was a coterie of other girls, all hair and teeth and eyelashes, all laughing at whatever Leo had said. Jessica recognised one of them as Anna from the other day in the canteen. *Cow*, she thought. *One minute she's all 'Oh poor you' to her friend, and the next she's all but spreading her own legs for the git.*

The group passed by without a glance at her and Anthony – maybe the invisible man's powers were rubbing off on her – and so she prepared herself to smile at Marco across the room. This could be it. Could be the moment. Eyes meeting across a crowded room and all that.

She flicked back her hair and fired her best smile.

But Marco was gone.

The table where he had been stood was now occupied by someone else. She looked around but there was no sign of him.

She cursed to herself. Typical. This always happened to her. Oh well, Anthony was still here.

She turned to Anthony. 'Any more of that special drink, sir?'

Anthony grinned and raised the silver flask. 'Certainly milady.'

He poured a generous shot into her cup. Then they toasted again, and she chugged a mouthful of the vodka-enriched orange juice. That hit the spot.

She smiled and started chattering to Anthony about the state of the canteen, and around her the party continued unabated.

11

While Jessica kept her wits about her, the days passed without much incident. The dance classes continued, and as Jessica's hip was feeling much better, she started to practice some of the more complex movements in order to strengthen herself for the main performance.

The classes were now being split up to take account of those who would be performing in *Appollon Musagete* and those who would not. This allowed them to work with each other on their movements, and to start to bring together the complex sequences that made up the ballet.

Thus Jessica found herself increasingly in classes with Leo, Rowan and Marco, as well as the others in the production. While she couldn't care less about Leo and Rowan, it was good to see Marco more regularly. He seemed a little shy, but she smiled at him when she saw him, and more than once caught him watching her.

She even plucked up the courage to ask him where he had disappeared to at the social.

'I saw you there, but then you were gone,' she said.

Marco just nodded and muttered something about needing to leave early that night. Jessica left it there, thinking that if she just treated it as casually as he was, then she wouldn't come over as some creepy stalker.

She shrugged and changed the subject to the ballet. Marco was doing pretty well all told as Hades. It was a good role, villain of the underworld and all that.

'What I'm not quite understanding,' she said, 'is where Hades comes into it all. The ballet as written doesn't contain that character.'

Marco nodded. 'I looked it up too. What they're doing is reworking some of the elements to provide roles for more of the dancers here. Apollo, of course, is the lead, and it's basically about his relationship with the Muses.'

'Yes. Calliope, Polyhymnia and Terpsichore. Rowan is dancing Calliope.'

'Yes, but the idea is that Apollo instructs them, and then leads them to Parnassus, their home. Along the way he is tempted and tormented by others – Hades included – until they arrive. This sequence comes in the *Pas de Deux* where Apollo duets with these characters as they travel.'

'Hmm.' Jessica could see how they could interpret the tableaux of the ballet in that way. 'Clever. I like that it gives more than just the four leads the chance to shine.'

Marco nodded. 'I know. It is a shame though that only the leads get their own variations. I would have loved to have performed a solo.'

Jessica smiled. 'Sometimes having a variation is not so good,' she commented. 'Think of the pressure. Just you on the stage, alone, dancing.'

As she spoke, Marco's eyes drifted off and Jessica could see that she was actually describing his dream. He grinned at her.

'Some of us long for that, you know,' he said.

'Well,' said Jessica, 'dancing Calliope isn't a walk in the park! It's quite hard maintaining the flow and posture as the music washes over and around you.'

'I've seen you,' said Marco. 'You're brilliant! There's true poetry in your movements, which is kinda apt given which Muse Calliope is.'

Jessica felt herself blush. She really wasn't used to getting compliments.

'Here comes trouble,' said Marco, and Jessica looked to see that Leo was approaching them from across the room. He was smiling, and that always meant that something was up.

'Hey Jessica,' he said as he reached them. 'Just wanted to say that you're doing really well. Glad that the hip is sorted now.'

Jessica smiled back, but inside she was wary and wondering what the problem was. There was always a problem where Leo was concerned.

'Thanks Leo,' she said.

Marco looked awkward. Leo had all his attention on Jessica, and it was as though he wasn't even in the room!

'I'll … I'll catch you later,' he said, and hurriedly made his way over to some other friends.

'Yeah, see you,' called Jessica.

Leo was still smiling at her.

'Was there something you wanted, Leo?' she asked sweetly.

'Yes, in fact there is,' he said. 'I've been watching you dance Calliope, and as we have some sequences together in the *Pas de Deux* and *Coda*, I wondered if you'd like to work on those with me.'

Jessica blinked. 'B … but I'm just the understudy. Rowan … she's–'

'Yeah, yeah … Rowan …' interrupted Leo. 'She's not a great one for rehearsal and practice.'

'I'd noticed,' said Jessica under her breath.

'So. I wondered if you had some time tonight?'

'Well … I …'

'Fantastic,' said Leo. 'Let's say eight o'clock, back here in this room. It's large enough for the movement, and we can work out how it should appear.'

'I … erm … okay,' said Jessica, somewhat startled by this turn of events. She wondered what Leo was up to.

'Great. See you later then,' Leo said, and wandered back off to his usual group of girls across the way.

Jessica watched him carefully, but they didn't giggle and look her way – a clear sign that they were setting her up for something. She frowned. It couldn't hurt to meet up – at least she would get the opportunity to dance with Leo – and he was a good dancer despite his arrogance.

At that moment Madame Rossi entered the room and clapped her hands together to get the assembled students' attention.

'Boys! Girls! Attention!'

Those assembled turned their attention to Madame Rossi, and the class began warming up. Jessica stretched her legs and arms, and continued to wonder what Leo's motivation was.

'What do you think?' asked Jessica as she chatted to Anthony over a coffee later in the day.

'I think he's a sleaze,' came the reply. 'But I guess he could be genuine on this. It's hard to tell, isn't it?'

Jessica nodded, and looked mournfully at the

twisting cream trail on top of her coffee. 'It's like my life, isn't it?'

'What is?'

'The pattern on my coffee. All twisty and turny and heading nowhere.'

'Now, look,' said Anthony, moving his stick so that he could lean closer. 'Just stop that now. There's nothing wrong with your life. You are doing what you always wanted to. To dance. And you're bloody good at it as well. So I don't want to hear talk like that.'

Jessica smiled at him. 'Sounds like I'm being told off,' she said.

'Too right,' said Anthony, bringing his fist down on the table in a mock show of anger. 'You're better than most of the students here and you know it. But unlike most of them, you don't go around bragging about it.'

Jessica nodded, her thoughts turning to her mysterious benefactor as they often did. She enjoyed meeting with him. Adored the attention he gave her. Was frankly *loving* the sex. And he was good for her dance tuition as well. But he never really *talked* to her. Thank goodness she had Anthony to bounce these things off as well.

She grinned at him and dipped her finger in the coffee. She stared intently at the cream on the end of her finger for a moment.

'What is it?' asked Anthony, leaning forward.

'Ha!' cried Jessica and tapped him on the nose with her creamy finger. There was a dab of coffee and white on his nose and he crossed his eyes to see.

'Why, you ...' he smiled, and wiped the end of his nose with his hand.

'Well, you cheered me up,' said Jessica. 'And I like that.'

'My pleasure. Just …'

'Just what?'

'Just be careful tonight, yes? Keep your eyes and ears open, and if he tries anything …'

Jessica nodded. 'Scream the place down.'

'You got it.'

The room was gloomy when Jessica arrived.

The usually bustling corridors of the Acadamie were quiet and empty, and Jessica wondered where everyone was. There was usually someone around.

She pushed open the door and stepped in. The room was illuminated only by the lights of a row of make-up tables to one side, and she could see them reflected in the floor-to-ceiling mirrors that lined the wall.

The door closed and clicked shut behind her.

'Leo?' she called.

There was a rustling sound from the far end of the room, and Leo emerged from the gloom and walked towards her. He was wearing a pair of dancer's tights and a close-fitting T-shirt that hugged his muscled torso closely.

Jessica could see his impressive manhood held by the tights and she hoped he was wearing a box.

'Jessica,' he said, sliding over to her with a deceptive grace. 'Thanks so much for coming along.'

Jessica flicked her eyes about. They seemed to be alone, so this wasn't some devious trick to embarrass her in front of everyone else. She spotted something resting in front of one of the make-up mirrors, and she peered more closely. It was a bandana … Peter had left it there perhaps.

She felt Leo touch her arm, and her attention shot back to him.

'That's fine, Leo,' she said. 'The ballet is quite complex and it's a good idea to try to get some practice in.'

'I'm so glad you agree,' he said, smiling a wolfish grin at her. 'And anyway, it gives us a chance to get to know each other a little.'

He turned and moved across to where a small CD player was placed. He stood and fiddled with the buttons for a moment.

Jessica watched him and couldn't help but admire the defined muscles of his butt as he crossed the floor. *Such a shame he's such an ass,* she thought. *He has* such *an ass!*

After a moment, Stravinsky's music played out, and Jessica instinctively felt herself relax and prepare to dance. There was something almost hypnotic about the music, and as she had rehearsed and practiced and listened to it over and over, she had trained herself into the right mindset for the performance. This was also something that her muse and lover had drilled into her – that to dance well, you had to relax into the music and let it lead and control you.

Leo turned and came to the middle of the room. He assumed a starting position, and as the music reached the right point, he started the sequence of moves that would bring him to where Jessica was stood. She went up *en pointe* and raised her arms, ready for the moment that they would meet.

She watched Leo as he smoothly spun and stepped towards her, his own muscular arms held in front of him, and his legs finding the rhythm.

They met, and she was whisked into his arms,

spun, and then the two of them danced around in a quarter circle before she was released, held by one hand, and then spun back into his embrace.

She could feel the heat from his hands on her skin. He was strong, and as they danced, they touched several times. Leo let his hands linger a little on her body, moving with the music and stroking her when he had the chance. Despite herself, she began to feel a little aroused.

She remembered this sequence from her practice with the masked man, and she felt that her stranger was a far better dancer than Leo was; but even so, Leo was pretty good.

At the end of the movement, Leo stumbled slightly and lost the rhythm.

'Damn,' he exclaimed under his breath. 'That's a hard one to get right.'

He returned to the CD player, and he and Jessica tried the sequence again. This time, Leo kept the flow, and they ended the sequence with him holding her by the hand, as she span away from him.

'That's good,' he said appreciatively. 'You move well, Jessica.'

'Thanks,' she smiled.

'Okay,' Leo said as he returned to the CD. 'Another one.'

This time, the dance was slower still, and Jessica recognised it as a piece from the *Coda*.

Leo moved sensuously, almost cat-like in his grace, as he circled Jessica, taking the steps in the ballet with precision and care. Jess watched him, one part of her mind liking the way his muscles rippled and moved under his unitard.

The movement ended with Calliope in Apollo's

arms, and so Jessica moved with Leo, circling him in turn, her movements matching his in the synchronicity that was needed for the overall piece to appear like perfect art to the audience.

As the music climaxed, so their movements ended with them in each other's arms.

The CD abruptly cut off, leaving them entwined together on the floor of the dance theatre.

Jessica's breathing stabilised, and she made to get up, but Leo held her down. He moved his head closer and she felt him nuzzle her neck gently.

'No. Leo. Please, no.'

But Leo was undeterred. He kissed her neck and stroked her arms gently with his hands.

'Jessica ...'

'Leo!' Jessica struggled a little, but in the position that she was, she could not really move until Leo released her.

'Jessica ... I've thought of this moment all year ...'

'What?' Jessica's head was a jumble of thoughts now. How could he have? She was a no-one. The proverbial ugly duckling in a pool of swans. Immediately she knew he was trying to spin his usual line. This time on her.

Leo breathed in and stroked her body.

'Say you haven't felt it. The connection between us?' he said.

Jessica shook her head. 'No. There's no connection. Nothing.'

'But surely ...?' Leo placed one hand on her stomach and held her there.

Jessica flashed back to all the times she had watched Leo in the downstairs room with his conquests. The things he would say to them ... the ways in which he expected them to respond. She had no intention of becoming another of his momentary playthings – broken and discarded when he had finished with his fun.

'Leo! No!' she shouted, and thrashed, breaking free of his hold and tumbling to the ground. She pushed herself up on one knee and looked him in the eyes. She was fuming now. How dare he treat her like that!

Leo, for his part, looked back at her calmly, a small smile flickering across his mouth.

'You think this is funny?' she spat. 'Just get out of here and leave me alone.'

Leo stood and watched her. 'I don't think so,' he said calmly.

Jessica pushed herself up onto her feet and stood a little unsteadily, watching him.

'What do you mean?'

'Well, Jessica,' Leo said, pacing slowly towards her again. 'I don't think you quite understand. I always get what I want. And tonight I want you. It's as simple as that.'

Jessica could not believe what she was hearing. Leo wanted her? She choked back a laugh. 'Me? You want me? Shit, Leo, you've had most of the girls here already. What makes me special?'

'You said no,' Leo replied calmly. 'And I love a challenge.'

'Okay,' Jessica said. 'That's enough Leo. I said no because I mean no.'

She made to stalk past him to the door but he caught her arm and swung her around again.

'You go when I say you can go.'

Jessica snarled at him and tried to pull her arm away, but he held her tight, his fingers biting into her flesh until she knew she would be bruised.

'Let me go!' she cried.

Leo just smiled his implacable smile and started to pull her across the room to where a couch sat against the far wall. Jessica's eyes widened. Surely he didn't hope to force her into sex with him on that, did he? He couldn't!

'What the fuck are you doing?'

She struggled and pushed her feet against the floor, but she couldn't gain any purchase there. They reached the couch and she refused to go back on it. She struggled and fought with Leo, but he was far stronger than she was, and she realised that this could be a battle that she was going to lose.

In her panic, she lost sight of what Leo was doing, and so the painful slap to her face took her completely by surprise. She fell back, stunned, onto the couch, and her hand raised to her cheek, which was still stinging.

Leo stood over her, a look of triumph on his face. 'So. You behave yourself and we have some fun, or I swear you'll never dance again.'

Jessica trembled at his words. They were a double-edged threat. Did he mean that he would hurt her so badly she would never be able to dance again? Or just that he would do his utmost to ruin her career. She didn't know how she was going to get out of this one.

'Now,' said Leo, a leer on his face. 'Let me see you _'

He bent down, ripping at her leotard. Jessica felt the fabric tear. His hands groped her. She pushed at them, nails scratching his skin until he delivered another, more forceful slap. Jessica yelped as much in fear and pain as in anger, but her continued struggles were useless against his strength.

Within minutes he was lying on top of her, yanking away the damaged fabric in order to gain better access to her breasts. She closed her eyes, all thought of fighting disintegrating with the last pull of the fabric. She felt her strength slipping away into her trembling limbs. She couldn't fight him. He was just too strong.

He was abruptly pulled backwards away from her, and Jessica wondered for a moment what had happened.

She sat up and saw that Leo was now lying on the ground, under another man who pulled back his fist and punched him hard in the face. Leo slumped back, stunned, and the newcomer stood and brushed his clothes down. He turned and stepped towards Jessica.

Jessica recognised the black and silver mask instantly, and she flew from the couch into his arms.

She instantly felt safe, and looked down at the prone form of Leo.

'He … he was going to rape me!'

'I know … I know …' said the stranger, stroking her hair with his hand. 'You should have been more careful.'

'I was as careful as I could be,' Jessica protested. 'I tried to be professional and nice, and to keep away from any issues … but he obviously had other ideas.'

The man nodded. 'I think we might need to ensure that Leo here is not of a mind to have anything to do with you again.'

Leo was stirring on the floor, shaking his head to try to clear it. Jessica could see that a trickle of blood from his nose was snaking down his face. He licked his lips and tasted the blood, winced and then wiped it from his face with the back of his hand.

The masked man let go of Jessica and moved towards Leo.

'You will leave her alone,' he said, his voice almost a whisper.

Leo looked up and cowered back, his legs involuntarily pushing him away from the masked and black-clad apparition before him.

'You will not touch her again.'

Leo nodded and sniffed. More blood trickled, and he wiped it off again.

'Now. Get up and go.'

The masked man took a warning step towards the cowed dancer, and Leo needed no further encouragement. He staggered to his feet and headed for the door, picking up his bag as he went. When he reached the door, his bravado returned for a moment and he turned and looked at Jessica and the man.

'No-one tells me what to do. You … both of you … will regret this.'

And with that he swept from the room, the door clunking shut behind him.

Jessica felt the tension leave her body in a wave, and she moved straight into the stranger's arms again, relaxing into him.

'Thank you,' she whispered.

The man held her tight and she could smell his sensual spicy musk. She nuzzled into him and looked up into his masked eyes. As usual they were calm and collected, and she could see herself reflected in them. She saw his mouth twitch into a slight smile, and before she could stop herself, she raised her head up and kissed him, long and tight on the mouth.

His hands caressed her back and held her, as the chaste kiss went on for what seemed like an age.

Then Jessica broke contact and relaxed back onto her feet. She could feel the emotions raging through her. Anger at Leo and the way he had treated her as though she was some sweet to be taken from the box, sampled and then spat into the bin. But also something else, a deep and throbbing emotion she was unfamiliar with. She felt safe, and warm, and appreciated. She felt together with the man in the mask. Whatever happened, she wanted that feeling to continue.

With a spark of surprise and pleasure, she realised that she cared deeply for the stranger. This man who had brought her to the height of pleasure so many times now, and who was watching her and protecting her as well.

Could this be love? She wasn't sure, but the thought scared her.

She nestled back into his arms and let herself drift as her heartbeat returned to normal. She would have to find out ... and she felt that it would be a discovery worth making.

12

Jessica returned to her room, her mind in confusion.

After her close encounter with Leo, and her rescue by the masked man, she kept replaying the evening over and over in her mind. She kept seeing Leo's impressive bulge as he walked towards her, his equipment barely concealed by the box and his tights. She recalled Peter's bandana by the mirror. She remembered Leo leering at her, holding her … and then she remembered being held by the stranger, letting herself go, and kissing him.

But after that, he had suggested she return to her room; she was tired from the dancing and from Leo's attack, and she needed to recover her strength.

With that, the man had faded into the shadows and vanished, as though he had never been there at all. But Jessica had still been able to smell his lingering scent, taste his lips. And she had also seen the splashes of Leo's blood on the wooden floor where he had fallen. So she hadn't imagined the whole thing.

But worse had been the way that the stranger had dismissed her. It had felt cold somehow, not right. She felt an ache deep inside her. Something that wasn't a physical pain, but more akin to an itch or a nagging feeling. It made her want to keep her mobile phone with her in case the stranger texted her.

She lay down on the bed, pulling the sheet over her as she let all of these conflicting thoughts and feelings wash over her still-trembling body. She wasn't an obsessive personality at all. She didn't collect things or eagerly trawl shops and websites looking for the next items to buy. She didn't even keep any books, preferring to read them once and then give them away to friends or charity shops. Her mind usually flitted from one thing to the next.

So why was she thinking more and more about the stranger? Thinking about how he touched her. How he smelt. How he loved her. She looked forward more and more to each of their encounters, and the time in between was becoming less and less of interest to her.

Jessica turned over and found a cool spot in the bed with her feet. She was very distracted by all this, and worried about it affecting her concentration in class. Certainly of late she had been daydreaming and not paying attention, missing vital instructions from the tutors. So far she had been able to cover it up, but it had all started to eat at her. She would always race from class to her phone, eager to see if there was a message. And if not, then she felt flat and deflated.

As she drifted off to sleep, she wondered if this was really what love felt like, or was it just a crush, a transient obsession …

Jessica's alarm woke her at eight the next morning. She blinked, bleary eyed, at the weak light coming through the curtains.

She stumbled out of bed and automatically headed

for the shower. She stood under the hissing jets of hot water for around ten minutes, loving the feel of the water and the heat as it sluiced through her long hair and down over her body. There was something about having a shower that she really loved. She recalled someone once telling her that the moving water created ozone in the air, and that was what made it so invigorating. She had no idea if this was true, but she loved having showers.

Later, she sat at her dressing table, drying her hair with the hairdryer, brushing and straightening it. She looked at herself in the mirror. There was something different about her. She stopped moving and looked into her own eyes. They did not flinch away like they normally did. She looked and felt more confident.

Jessica smiled and watched as her mirror self did the same. She had a nice smile, she decided. Not crooked and weak as she had always thought, but pretty and strong.

She resumed brushing out her hair, and liked the sight of the girl in the mirror doing the same.

She still felt the same inside, but changed somehow. She felt stronger, more resilient, like she could take over the world. She remembered the masked man telling her that she needed to grow a pair … Crude, but an effective analogy. She couldn't go through life being the victim. She was better than that.

She looked down at her desk where her diary was lying. She had written her name on the front when she had first got it, and the book was partially covered by her straighteners.

All she could see was the start of her name: JESS.

It seemed to be a sign. Jessica said the name to herself, her lips moving imperceptibly. *Jess.*

She liked the contraction and for a moment

wondered why she had never thought of it before. She was the new Jess, not the old girly and unsure Jessica.

She finished off her hair and checked it in the mirror. Straight and glossy and gorgeous. She topped it off with a clip in the side to keep it from her eyes. She could change it to the regulation ponytail for the classes using the scrunchies she kept in her purse.

'You seem different,' said Anthony over their morning coffee.

Jess smiled and played innocent. 'Do I?'

'Yes.' Anthony looked at her closely. 'Have you done something with your hair?'

Jess stroked it with her hand. 'Maybe,' she said coyly.

'What is it?' asked Anthony. 'Anything I should know?'

'No,' said Jess. 'I feel great, that's all. I woke up this morning feeling very happy and confident.'

'You should get out of that side of the bed more often,' smiled Anthony.

'Cheeky,' said Jess, punching him on the arm. 'I don't know, I just feel … more alive somehow.'

'There is certainly a gleam in your eye,' said Anthony. 'What's causing that, I wonder? All those secret assignations with your mystery man perhaps?'

'Maybe …'

'It is … I can see it in your face!'

Jess looked at Anthony. 'I'm worried though.'

'About what?'

'Well … about … you know. I think I have … feelings … for the man. Even though I have no idea who he is, or even what he looks like under the mask.'

'Feelings?'

Jess nodded. 'He's kind to me, and sensitive. He seems to know what I want and what I like ... He's a good teacher ...' she smiled again '... in more ways than one.'

'But you have no idea who he is,' said Anthony thoughtfully.

'Not a clue,' said Jess. 'He wears a mask all the time, his hair is slicked back so there's no clue there. His body doesn't have any tattoos or scars that might give the game away ... He's a mystery.'

'... and an enigma,' smiled Anthony.

'... a mystery wrapped in an enigma,' added Jess.

'... and bloody good in bed by all accounts!'

Jess blushed. 'Yes,' she nodded. 'He is fucking good!'

Anthony nodded. 'I can see the problem. If you find out who he is, then you're worried that it might all end?'

'I'd not thought of that,' said Jess. 'But yes, that does worry me. Also that if I find out who he is, then the passion might go away. How much of it is all the thrill of not knowing, and how much is real and genuine ?'

Anthony reached over and took her hand. She was trembling slightly.

'Poor you,' he said. 'I don't have anything I can really give you. I've been keeping an eye out, watching your back, but everything seems safe and above board – well, as above board as clandestine sex with a complete stranger can be!'

Jess laughed, and Anthony squeezed her hand.

'There you are. I like to hear you laugh.'

Jess smiled at him. 'I know I'm probably worrying about all the wrong things, but the ballet is so important, and I want to make a good impression. Plus I love the way he looks at me, how he holds me and loves me, as though I am the most precious piece of china, and that if he isn't careful I might break. That couldn't be faked, could it?'

Anthony thought for a moment, looking into her earnest eyes. 'I don't think so, Jessica. It sounds like maybe you're concerned over nothing, but equally, it pays to be cautious. So the only advice I can give is to keep doing what you are doing … but be careful … and be alert.'

'… because Britain needs lerts!' finished Jess with a smile.

Anthony laughed at that, and Jess grinned at him.

'Oh, and another thing. I've decided I want to be called Jess from now on. Jessica was the old me. Jess is the new. I feel stronger and better and more confident. So Jess, if you please, sir?'

Anthony made a mock bow in his seat. 'Of course milady,' he said. 'Jess it shall be.'

Jess checked her watch, noted the time, and her eyebrows shot up.

'Oh Christ, I'm late!'

She grabbed her bag and slurped down the last of her coffee.

'Thanks Anthony! As usual you have a way of putting everything into perspective for me.'

She kissed him on the cheek and hurried off across the café towards the door. Anthony watched her go, then lifted himself gingerly off the seat and hobbled to the door on his stick.

In the hallway, Jess raced through the students who were thronging there. She was late for her next class and had no wish to fall foul of her tutors' discipline at this stage.

She turned a corner and spotted Marco from the corner of her eye. He was carrying one of the sandbags used to prop up the sets on stage, making his way toward the basement where they were stored. Distracted, she turned her head to watch him, and cannoned into a girl who was stood in a group with three others just around the corner.

The girl dropped her folder and papers flew everywhere.

'Oh my God, I'm so sorry,' blurted Jess, and automatically started to pick the papers up.

'Fucking hell, you retard!' came a voice. 'Why don't you just watch the fuck where you're going?'

Jess looked up and saw that the girl she had bumped into was Natalie. As she met her blazing eyes it was like falling into a well. She could hear laughter, and the girls were all looking at her.

She stammered and stumbled again as she rose, hopelessly pushing the papers into Natalie's hands.

'I ... I ... I'm sorry,' she managed, before she turned and hurried off down the corridor, chased by a cacophony of laughter and cat calls.

Jess choked back tears of embarrassment. How could she ever live this down ...? She was disappointed with herself. Clearly she wasn't as strong and confident as she had thought.

As she passed the stairwell she didn't see a figure stood in the shadows. He had seen everything, from the accident to the way the girls had treated Jess. He shook his head and his long finger touched the bottom of the mask covering the upper part of his face. Jess would need some further help in this area, he felt.

As Jess's back vanished down the corridor, the

stranger turned and made his way downstairs to the basement area. There were some things he needed to prepare.

13

Jess received the text as she left the Acadamie's secretarial offices at the end of classes for the day. She had popped in to sign the appropriate forms to change her name from 'Jessica' to 'Jess' on the records. She hoped that this would help with the transition from the old her to the new.

'8 PM, BASEMENT AREA.'

Jess smiled with anticipation. As usual it was unsigned, but she knew the number it came from, and knew that she would be in for a good time.

First, though, she popped into the canteen and picked up a couple of pastries and a cup of coffee to snack on. After an afternoon dancing and exercising, she needed the quick calories from something sugary.

Then it was back to her room to shower, change and prepare herself for the evening's session … and she could only guess at what her masked teacher might have in store for her.

Jess pushed open the door of the unused basement room and stepped in. Everything seemed in place. The couch was there in the middle of the room, the holes in the plaster giving a view into the other room that Leo liked to use … nothing was out of place.

Jess looked around. It wasn't like her teacher to be late. She checked her watch. It was eight on the nose. She sighed. She would just have to wait.

Her eyes fell on a carton that had been left on the couch. She went over to it and saw her name neatly printed on a card resting on the top.

Jess picked the card up and turned it over. Printed on the reverse was an instruction: 'PUT THIS ON.'

She looked again at the box. It was standard cardboard with no markings on it. She opened the top, lifting the flaps to peer inside. She could see nothing but some deep red tissue paper, so she put her hand in to move it out of the way.

Under the paper, her hand encountered something cool and smooth. She let her fingertips play over the surface of whatever it was for a moment, then put both hands into the box and pulled free the contents.

It spilled out over the couch and almost slid through her fingers. It was some sort of shiny material, a deep burgundy red colour. Jess couldn't make out what it was though, so she pulled it up and held it before her. The material was glossy, and as she held the top in her hands, the rest fell to the floor, revealing it to be a catsuit made of a smooth, shiny and soft latex material. There was a zipper extending right down the back, and Jess could see that it had gloves and feet included in the design.

Jess let out her breath and realised that she had been holding it in. She shook her head and wondered how one was supposed to get into such an outfit. She had never worn anything like it before.

She remembered back to a Halloween party a few years earlier when she had gone as a cat – with whiskers and cat-nose drawn on her face with eyebrow pencil, and wearing a cotton catsuit, complete with tail, and an Alice band with little cat ears on her head. But that had been simple party wear. This was something else entirely. This was fetish. She wasn't sure how she felt about that.

Jess held the suit in her hand and looked closer. The zipper up the back slid down easily enough, and Jess noticed that it actually extended under the crotch and up the stomach area as well. There were also three zipper pulls built into the fastening. Jess wondered why that might be, but for the moment left them all at the stomach area, leaving the back and legs open.

The material was smooth and yet strangely warm in her fingers, and she realised that the heat from her hands was being transferred to the material.

She smoothed her hand over it. There was little resistance. It was shiny and sleek.

Oh well, she thought. *In for a penny …*

Checking quickly that the door was closed, Jess stripped off her leggings and skirt, leaving herself naked from the waist down.

She had shaved her pussy again, so it was smooth and hairless, and she still felt good about herself.

She sat on the couch and lifted the catsuit again, figuring out which way round it went, and which leg went where. Then, with a breath, she slid one leg into the leg of the suit.

Almost immediately she could feel the cool latex encase her leg. It felt good, and she wiggled her ankle and toes to get her foot down into the bottom. She then pulled the latex up her leg, loving how it swished and felt against her skin.

Then she slipped her other leg into the suit. This also felt amazing, so she pulled the latex material up her thighs. She then turned her attention to the zipper.

She realised that with three zipper pulls, she could be completely enclosed in the suit, and also have access to her intimate parts via the middle opening. She smiled. This would be very interesting indeed.

She positioned the front zip, closing up that section of the suit, and did likewise with the middle one. This left the final zip for the back, and this she left open. Jess pulled the suit up over her bottom, loving how the latex stretched and gripped her. Initially cool on her skin, but then rapidly warming up as the heat from her body entered the material.

Jess pulled off her T-shirt and bra – thinking idly that wearing nice underwear that evening had been a waste of time – and pulled the suit up her torso. She manoeuvred one arm into the space for it, and then the other, pulling and tugging at the tight material to get her fingers into the attached gloves, and wiggling her body to encourage the material up and over her torso.

Eventually she had the suit in place over her shoulders. It was tight, and looking down, Jess could see the dim lights reflecting in the glossy surface.

She wondered how she would get the back done up, and twisted her arm around her lower back to grasp the zipper pull there. She managed to tug it half way up her back before her arm would move no further.

She relaxed for a moment.

The suit felt amazing on. It was smooth and sleek, and hugged all her curves perfectly. She felt enclosed and somehow safe.

'You look very good,' came a voice, and Jess

turned with a start.

The masked stranger was stood by the door. He had obviously entered while she had been dressing.

'Why, thank you,' Jess smiled. 'I am having a little trouble here though …'

The man moved towards her and Jess turned her back on him. 'Could you?'

He grasped the zipper pull, and Jess felt the most incredible sense of erotic power as the zip closed up her back. She felt the catsuit grip her body as it went. The suit held her tightly, enclosing her.

Her breasts were gripped by the sheer material and the fabric tightened and held her tiny waist. Finally, her shoulders, upper arms and neck felt the kiss of the latex as the zip was closed to the very top.

Jess blinked, and a shudder of pleasure went through her.

'How's that?' asked the man.

'It's … it's amazing,' said Jess, stretching herself like a cat.

'There's one final piece,' said the stranger, reaching back into the box.

His hand emerged with a smaller object, also made from the burgundy latex. It was a hood, Jess noted, and she turned to look at the man.

'You want me to wear that as well?'

'If you want to …'

Jess nodded and held out her gloved hand for the headpiece.

She turned it around, working out how it went – there was a mask-like area at the front with holes for her eyes, nose and mouth, and at the back there was a further hole through which her hair could emerge.

She placed the mask over her head and teased her

hair out the back. The stranger helped her, lifting her hair out and through the mask as she positioned it correctly on her head.

When she had finished, she turned and looked at the man. 'How do I look?'

'See for yourself,' he said. Taking her hand, he led her over to one side of the room, where a full-length mirror was hung.

Jess looked and for a moment could not understand what she was seeing.

In front of her was some fetish goddess in burgundy latex. The tight material defined every element of her body, enhancing her curves. The material shone in the dim light as she turned to see the details. Her legs seemed strong and sensual, and her flat stomach and thighs framed her pussy, which was defined under the latex, and bisected by the lower zip. Her body curved in at the waist, and then her breasts pushed out against the material at her chest. She could even see the excited nubs of her nipples pressing against the taut material. She ran her hands over her body, and marvelled at the way the latex felt. She felt incredibly sexy.

The stranger moved closer, and in the mirror she could now see them side by side. She was a masked cat-woman. Her eyes were sharp, and her long, red hair cascaded down her back from the head mask, perfectly set off by the burgundy of the suit. He meanwhile remained the sexy, enigmatic character she had come to know and love.

She whistled gently. 'Is that really me?' she asked.

The stranger nodded beside her. 'It is.'

'My God,' said Jess. 'I'm like some sort of fetish wet dream!'

She stroked her hands over her body again, and noted that her breasts perked up when she ran her fingers over her nipples. She enjoyed the feeling of her own hands pressing the latex against her skin.

'This is amazing,' she said, turning to the masked stranger. 'So what do we do now, go and fight crime together?'

The man smiled. 'Well, we could if you wanted to, I suppose. But I rather thought that I'd leave what happens now up to you.'

'What do you mean?' asked Jess.

'Well … how do you feel?' he asked.

Jess thought for a moment, still admiring her body in the tight catsuit in the mirror.

'I feel … strong,' she said. 'And powerful. As though I am totally in control.'

The man nodded. 'And what do strong, powerful women do?'

Jess felt a frisson pass through her body, and the tight latex around her pussy seemed to tighten further. 'They take what they want,' she whispered, half to herself.

'So what do you want?'

Jess flicked her eyes from her reflection to the man stood next to her.

'You,' she said. 'I want you.'

The man smiled, and started to back away to the couch.

'So take what you want,' he said.

Jess stepped forward, loving the way that the catsuit moved with her, hugging her close and making her feel … unstoppable. She walked towards him, and even her stride had changed, as she tipped her hips from side to side. She felt the latex working between her thighs, rubbing her clitoris, and she felt the dampness there.

'Well,' she said coyly, 'as you put it like that ...'

She reached the spot where the masked man waited, then placed her hand on his chest. With a slight pressure she pushed him back, and he fell seated onto the couch.

She lithely ran her gloved hand through his hair, moving it down across his masked cheek, and ran her finger across his lips.

'Shhhhh,' she said.

Jess then turned her attention to his body. She stroked her hands down his chest and found the buckle of the trousers he was wearing. She looked up into his eyes, cocking her head to one side, and swiftly undid the buckle, unzipping him too with one smooth movement.

Jess was pleased when he let out a moan of pleasure – often he was silent during their trysts – and he lifted his bottom to allow her to slide his trousers off. Maybe tonight she would really make *him* let go.

Jess's hands then smoothed over his bare legs and up to his boxer shorts. She let them hover teasingly over his crotch, and then gently touched him there, noting with pleasure that he was large and erect. Not that this was ever a problem.

She hooked her thumbs into his boxers and tugged them down as well, taking them and the trousers off and tossing them aside.

She kept her eyes fixed on his eyes as she let her hands slide and caress around his thighs, letting them stroke against his balls every so often. Then she slid them around his balls and up his shaft, gently holding him and stroking him with the warm latex.

She looked down and was again impressed at his

size. Certainly more than enough to please any girl.

She smiled and gently wanked his cock with one hand, while the other teased him under his balls, stroking him there and making him squirm.

'What is it you want my darling?' Jess asked, wanting to make him beg all of a sudden. There was something about the latex catsuit that brought something of the devil out in her. She loved how it felt and how it made her feel.

The man moaned gently again, and looked her in the eye. 'You … I want you …'

Jess smiled and chuckled gently to herself. 'Oh, you shall have me, never fear,' she said. 'But first … first I need to make sure you are ready …'

She stopped moving her hands over him, and smiled up at him.

'Shall I begin?'

The man swallowed and nodded. 'Oh Christ yes,' he said.

With that, Jess lowered her head and licked up the length of his cock with her tongue. He was salty, but that sensual musky smell was there, and she breathed in. She loved how this man smelt, and she had to taste him now. She realised as she did so that she had never taken his cock in any place other than her pussy. It was something she was about to rectify.

She lifted his large cock to her lips and kissed him on the tip. Then she extended her tongue and gently licked around the head before pulling it into her mouth and sucking the end like a lollipop. She licked, kissed and sucked for a few moments, and then slowly let his length sink into her mouth, all the time moving her tongue around his shaft.

He moaned louder, and Jess smiled around his

cock. She loved that reaction. She proceeded to move her mouth up and down on his cock, gently stroking him with her hand at the same time. Jess hadn't had that much experience in this department, but the mask and the costume made her feel so confident that she let instinct lead her through it. His cock filled her mouth. It made her want him in her pussy at the same time. She felt excited by his taste, and as she sucked him, a small amount of pre-cum leaked onto her tongue. She drew back and swallowed, loving the taste of him.

She was determined that this was a blow job he would remember.

She alternated her strokes. Sometimes with her hand, sometimes with her mouth. She was servicing this magnificent cock to the best of her ability, and she felt so strong and in control.

She looked up at his masked face. His eyes were closed in pleasure, and his hands were gently stroking her shoulders. She loved the feel of his hands on the latex, and how that feeling transferred to her skin underneath.

She slowly and lasciviously sucked and licked at his engorged cock, bathing it in her saliva. He moaned again, and she could hear that his breathing was becoming more ragged. She lifted her mouth from him and firmly stroked his penis with her hand. She saw a bead of clear fluid emerge from the eye and she smiled. She moved her finger and collected it, using the lubrication to smooth over the head of his cock.

'What do you think, my darling?' she asked in a low voice. 'Are you ready for me now?'

The man looked down at her, and she could see the need in his eyes.

'I can see that you are,' she said.

She pulled back from him and stood before him, a goddess in tight, shiny latex, eyes blazing and with red hair cascading down her back.

She ran her hands over her breasts, squeezing them through the tight covering, and slid them down her stomach to her pubis, performing a little wiggle and dip from the knees at the same time. She licked her lips as she saw the need turn to desperation.

'You like me like this,' she purred, letting her hands cup her pussy gently.

'You want me to …?' she asked, letting one hand toy with the zipper pull just below her belly button.

The man nodded and licked his own lips. Eyes fixed on her hand where it held the zipper.

She smiled and slowly pulled the zip down, revealing her creamy flesh below the smooth latex material. As she pulled it lower, so her hairless pussy came into view, and the man gasped as she pulled the zip down and under, revealing herself to him.

'Oh, so you like what you see … Well …'

Jess smoothed her hands over her body again. She really couldn't get enough of the suit, and the touch of the latex gloves felt so sexy on her excited clit.

She moved closer to the stranger, and his hands came out to touch her. He held her around the waist, and small electric charges went off in her skin where he touched her through the latex. He stroked her gently, and she manoeuvred herself into position over him on the couch.

She reached down and caught his cock in her hand, moving it so that the head rested against the entrance to her pussy. Then she held the back of the couch as he supported her waist, and lowered her pussy down on his cock slowly.

She looked down and saw his length being swallowed by her other lips, and gasped involuntarily at the feeling of being totally filled. She was so wet that there was no resistance at all, and she slid firmly down to the base of his member.

Fuck, he's a big boy, she thought to herself as she raised herself up slightly, and then plunged down once more.

With every stroke, the passage became wetter and easier. The temptation to just throw herself wildly into it was immense, but she held herself back. Control was the key word here, and she wanted the man to feel every part of her control over him.

She smiled to herself and started to bounce more quickly up and down on his cock. The feeling was exquisite, and she bit her lip gently with the pleasure.

The man had his hands holding her waist, but otherwise he was in her power completely. She could feel him trying to buck up into her, but she slowed her movements again, and teased him with long, slow strokes, taking him as deep as he could go each time. She experimented with tightening her muscles on the outward stroke, and heard him moan in pleasure each time she did that.

'You like that, baby?' she whispered in his ear.

'Yes,' he moaned. 'Oh, fuck yes.'

So she did it some more, alternating her speed, slowing every time he seemed to be reaching a peak, and then building him back up again.

After a minute or so of this, his hands were roaming over her latex-clad waist and arms, stroking and enjoying her as much as she was enjoying him. She pumped up and down faster, feeling his cock swell inside her. She could feel the beginnings of an orgasm herself now, and so slowed slightly and shifted position so that the head of his cock rubbed against her sensitive g-spot. She rocked back and forth, her mane of red hair tossing, as she felt herself crest and start squeezing and pulsing against him as she came.

As she cried out in pleasure, so this tipped the stranger over the edge and he tensed and came deep inside her, his cock throbbing and jerking as his hot seed flooded her pussy. They both enjoyed their orgasms, and slowed as they came down from the high. Jess could feel his cock still hard inside her, and sighed with pleasure as she rested, the stranger still deeply embedded within her.

Then, she lifted herself off, and his cock sprang free with a slight sucking sound, leaving Jess feeling empty. She kissed the stranger on the mouth, her tongue probing through the slit in her mask. He accepted her tongue, and they enjoyed a long and sensuous kiss together, his hands roving over her body and cupping the back of her head.

Jess pushed herself back and stood over him again. She could feel emptiness inside her. She looked at his cock, which was still erect.

'Interesting,' she said, trailing a finger down his belly and up, along his cock. 'Seems you're not finished yet.'

He smiled. 'What is your wish?' he asked.

Jess thought for a moment and sashayed around the couch. 'I think,' she said. 'I'd like you again.'

The man pushed himself off the couch and stood watching her, his big cock waving proudly in front of her.

Jess walked around the couch, loving the way that the catsuit felt, her skin in contact with the latex. She felt so powerful and in control that she might explode. No wonder superheroes wore this sort of stuff; it made you feel invincible, invulnerable.

She stopped in front of the man, then span on her toes, facing away from him. She bent forwards over the couch, then looked back at the stranger watching her.

'Come on then, lover boy. What are you waiting for? I want you to fuck me. Hard.'

The man needed no more encouragement, and he stepped behind her, his cock bobbing against her pussy entrance. His hands stroked the tight latex over her buttocks and thighs, and he braced himself.

Jess was feeling wild, and couldn't wait to be taken again. When his big cock started to progress into her pussy, it was as though she had never had anything so good before.

In this position, the underside of the man's penis gently stroked against her clitoris on every inward stroke, and his balls gently patted her once he was fully in. He could then withdraw slowly, his cockhead rubbing against her most sensitive spot. She felt herself going into a world of pleasure, where all sensation was focused on her cunt and the cock servicing it magnificently. She scrabbled on the couch as a small orgasm ripped through her, making her gasp and bathing the cock in more juices.

The man started to speed up, taking control of her body as she had controlled his. Jess shuddered as another orgasm ripped through her, making her gasp with pleasure and moan out that she was cumming as he continued to pump steadily and rhythmically into her.

Jess's whole world contracted to the lightning bolts of pleasure that were shooting from her pussy to the rest of her body. Her hands clenched the couch, and for a moment Jess wasn't even sure where she was. She thrashed her head from side to side and caught sight of her reflection in the mirror again. A beautiful, statuesque, gleaming latex woman, bent over and being serviced by a gorgeous man with the biggest cock ... She could even see his length as he pumped her over and over, and she could see his hands as he ran them over her back and waist as though he couldn't quite believe what was happening.

She closed her eyes in pleasure as the biggest orgasm yet hit her.

'Oh ... oh ... oh my God,' she cried. 'You're ... you're making me cum again!'

And with that she was lost. All awareness of the real world was ripped away as the pleasure and sensation coursed through her. It was like being plugged into an electric socket. All her senses closed down, and she slumped to the couch as her pussy convulsed and came over and over again on the cock that was working her there.

The man slowed down, sensitive to her needs, and allowed her to crest the waves of pleasure. She drew in a huge gasp and breathed again as awareness started to return to her. At that moment she felt him cumming again, and it pleased her that he was so excited he could no longer hold back.

She pushed herself up, and the man's cock slipped from her again. She was soaking wet down there, and feeling very, very satisfied. She turned and slumped on the couch, her breath racing. She concentrated and started to bring it back under control again, using the breathing techniques from her training to slow her heartbeat and to get herself back under control.

'Oh. My. God,' she said, once she could talk. 'That

was … amazing!'

The stranger smiled, and turned to where his boxers and trousers had been thrown. He slipped them back on, and although Jess was feeling totally relaxed and fulfilled, she suffered a pang of loss as the amazing cock was hidden again from view.

He sat down next to her on the couch and stroked the catsuit material appreciatively.

'I take it you like my little gift, then?'

Jess looked at him, her eyes shining under the mask. 'Oh, I *love* it,' she said. 'It makes me feel so … so sexy.'

'And strong,' said the man.

Jess nodded. 'Oh yes.'

'So. You need to remember that feeling,' the stranger said. 'Remember what it feels like to be wearing the suit, to be enclosed like this. To be in control.'

Jess nodded.

'Also, remember how the mask feels.' The man touched his own mask briefly. 'Wearing a mask allows us to behave in ways that we might not normally. It's like the characters in the ballet, in the dance. We take on their characteristics and they in turn allow us to live out some fantasies. So remember what it feels like to have the mask on, to be above what others feel or think, to be someone else for the duration.'

The man touched Jess's latex-covered cheek with his knuckles.

'You are so beautiful and talented,' he said. 'We will put that to good use here.'

Jess smiled. 'Thank you,' she said. 'Thank you for teaching me. For loving me. For believing in me.'

'Until next time then, *ma chérie*.'

The stranger stood and performed an elaborate

bow to Jess, before turning and striding across the room to the door. He opened it and left the room.

As the door clicked shut, Jess released a huge breath of air. She had been holding it again.

Wow she thought. *What did I just do!*

She stood and walked lithely over to the mirror again, admiring her figure once more. She stroked herself, still not quite believing that the Amazon she could see had once been meek, shy little Jessica.

She also thought on what the man had said just before he left. It was true that wearing this outfit and mask made her stronger, more daring, more confident. She had to take that, and continue with that feeling and attitude even when she wasn't dressed up. Could she do that? She looked into her own eyes reflected in the mirror and thought that perhaps she could.

14

Jess was awakened by something of a commotion in the corridor outside her room. There were raised voices, and a lot of movement.

She grabbed her gown and, struggling into it, cracked open her door to see what was happening.

She blinked in the light and could see other people looking out of their rooms too, all disturbed by whatever it was that was going on.

People were talking, but no-one seemed to have a clue. Jess left her room and followed some others out to the landing area that overlooked the main atrium of the Acadamie. There she could hear raised voices, and she pushed through some people to the balcony so that she could see what was going on.

Below her was another group of students, all standing in a circle around two figures. It was almost like an old-style playground fight, where the kids circle those battling, and chant 'Fight, fight, fight' until one of the teachers arrives to break it all up.

The two people in the middle, however, were not fighting physically. On one side was Leo, dressed in dance leggings and T-shirt. On the other was Rowan. She was wearing a pair of baggy sweatpants and a loose blouse. She was also shouting angrily at Leo.

'… fuck I'll keep quiet. You total shit. You bastard!'

Rowan was brandishing a mobile phone in her hand, and she shook it at Leo.

'You know what I found! Messages, that's what. Messages from other girls.'

Leo stepped towards her. 'And what were you doing snooping on my phone in the first place, Rowan?'

'I was looking for a number,' she retorted.

'What number? You have all the numbers you need.'

'Plus!' she screamed in his face. 'Plus, someone tipped me off that you might be playing around behind my back.'

Leo looked shocked. 'Babe. You know I would nev–'

'Yeah, right,' she interrupted.

Jess looked around the crowd and noticed a few of the girls pulling themselves back from the front, faces red. Among them were Anna and Yvette. Jess nodded to herself. Well the cat was out of the bag this time.

'You are such a shit, Leo. Listen to this: "Oh my darling, I can't wait to make love with you again. You are amazing!" An amazing liar, that is!'

Leo stepped forward again and made to take the phone from Rowan, but she skipped away.

'No you don't. If you think I'm too much of a lady to land a kick between your legs … then you're wrong. So keep back, scumbag.'

She looked up and around at her audience. 'Here's another: "You rock my world! I came so much last night. When can we meet again?" So which one of you was that from, then?'

She brandished the phone like a torch, holding it out and swinging it around the faces of the assembled crowd.

Leo was trying to regain his composure. 'Why are you believing all this rubbish?' he said. 'Rowan, I've seen no-one but you!'

'Liar!' she spat. 'You know, Leo, I've had it with you. You and your selfish ways, your lovers and your spats. I've had it!'

She turned and stalked away across the atrium. The eyes of all the assembled students were on her. She stopped and looked back.

'There's a message here about meeting you in the basement … The basement, eh? Is that where all your little secrets are hiding? I wonder what I'll find if I go down there?'

She turned and headed for the stairs that led down. As she reached them, still fuming, she turned and shouted at Leo. 'You will pay for this!'

At that moment, Anthony appeared out of a door on the other side of Rowan. Jess could see him look confused and say Rowan's name. Rowan span to look at him at the same moment as she started down the stairs. In her distraction she didn't see the sandbag placed on the second step down. Her foot glanced off it, and suddenly she lost her balance and was falling down the stairs, head over foot.

The hallway went silent all of a sudden,. The only sound was that of Rowan crumpling to the bottom of the stairs.

Someone screamed, and there was a flurry of movement as Anthony headed down the stairs himself, one step at a time, helped by his stick.

One of the teachers came running from the offices.

'Someone call an ambulance,' she shouted, and headed down the steps after Anthony.

A murmur started up as the students talked to each other in hushed tones. Below Jess, Marco hurried to the stairwell and shouted down that he had called for an ambulance and that help was coming.

Jess couldn't believe what had just happened. She stood looking over the balcony as the other students drifted off. Downstairs, Leo was left alone in the atrium with a look of defeat and terror on his face. He was trembling slightly. Jess could not feel sorry for him though. This had been coming for a long time now.

As the sound of an ambulance siren approached, Jess made her way back to her room. Her thoughts were on Rowan and whether or not she was going to be okay.

A couple of hours later, Madame Rossi called for Jess. She left her class and made her way to the office, wondering what the summons might be about. She hoped it wasn't anything to do with her little assignation with Leo ... Who knew what shit he might have been flinging around following Rowan's accident?

At the office door, she drew in a breath and rapped sharply.

'Come!'

She pushed opened the door and entered the office. Madame Rossi was there along with Miss Mathias and Miss Johns.

'Ah, Jessica Thomson, come in.'

Jess smiled and made her way to the chair. 'Ah, it's Jess, Madame.'

Madame Rossi smiled. 'Yes of course, Jess.'

Jess sat down and smiled at the three woman,

wondering what it was all about.

'So, how can I help you?' she asked.

'Well … Jess … you know that Rowan had something of a nasty fall today?'

'Yes, I did. Is she all right?'

'The poor dear has broken her leg. She slipped on the stairs and took a tumble, and broke something on the way down. She'll be out of action for some time, I'm afraid.'

'Oh no, that's awful,' said Jess.

'It is indeed,' said Madame Rossi. 'And more so because we have various things in track at the moment that we cannot delay.'

Jess nodded. She assumed they were talking about the staging of the ballet.

Madame Rossi confirmed this. 'The new ballet you have all been rehearsing. Well, the dates for that have all been booked in now, and we have investors and students coming along … so we can't really put it off.'

'I see,' said Jess.

'So, Jess,' said Madame Rossi, 'as you are the understudy for Rowan, we'd like you to step up and take her role in the production.'

Jess only half heard what Madame Rossi said. Surely they hadn't just offered her the female lead?

'I'm sorry,' she said. 'Did you just ask …?'

'Yes indeed,' said Miss Mathias. 'We have all been very impressed by your progress, even more because of your injury.'

The ladies were all smiling encouragingly at Jess, and she swallowed.

'Oh my. That's … Thank you … If you think I'm …'

'We do,' smiled Madame Rossi. 'And we would

like you to dance for us this afternoon. As you know, we have a run-through of the various elements of the ballet in today's class. Normally, you would be working with the Chorus as usual, but today we need you to take over as Calliope.'

Jess felt a sense of power wash over her. Previously she would have been shy, painful to the point of being unable to speak, but she knew that the dance was hers. She had been training with her lover most evenings, and she knew the sequences by heart. She was feeling more confident too, able to hold her own.

She thought back to the other night, when she had been wearing the latex catsuit and mask, the power and invincibility they had seemed to bestow. She remembered what her lover had said to her, to remember the feeling and to call on it when she needed. She smiled.

'I would be delighted, Madame Rossi,' she said. 'I just feel so bad for poor Rowan. She will be okay, won't she?'

'She will,' said Madame Rossi. 'The break is apparently clean and will heal, but it will take months before she can dance again. And we need you to fill in.'

'Between you and us, Jess,' said Miss Johns conspiratorially, 'we think you are better than Rowan anyway. In the last few weeks, we have watched you grow and blossom in class. Your technique has improved, as have your confidence and strength. To be honest, if we were casting today, you would be offered the lead anyway.'

Jess felt a smile cross her face. This was amazing!

'Thank you so much,' she said. 'I won't let you down.'

'It's our pleasure, Jess,' said Madame Rossi. 'So,

we'll see you this afternoon …'

'Yes. Thank you again.'

Jess got up and went to the door. She nodded her thanks again to the tutors and left the room. In the corridor outside, she leaned back against the wall and smiled even wider. She had done it. She had the lead in the ballet. Everything her confidante and lover had told her had come to pass …

She pushed herself away from the wall and made her way to the canteen to grab something before the afternoon's session. There was a new spring in her step, and she felt better than she had ever done before. She couldn't wait.

15

As the music started, Jess lifted her leg and made a gentle pass with her *pointe*, then stepped forward into the dance sequence.

Leo was stood beside her. Gracefully she slipped one arm through his, and he lifted her over his back slowly to land on the other side of him, allowing her to move into the standing splits that effortlessly segued into another lift around.

Stravinsky's music was mellow and slow, and the dance followed it. Jess was feeling the music with every step, and letting her heart and soul join with the sounds and the movement it evoked.

Leo was concentrating hard. After the events of that morning, he didn't want to be the next to be dropped from the production, due to not being good enough. He had taken the news about Rowan quite hard – obviously there was some part of him that had feelings and a heart, even if he kept it well locked down – but had reacted to Jess's promotion surprisingly well.

Jess thought that it was more that he was presented with a *fait accomplis* and had no choice. After all, there wasn't another girl in the Acadamie who knew the ballet and the steps … and that was the whole purpose of having an understudy, wasn't it?

Leo and Jess moved through the movements of the ballet. Jess spun slowly *en pointe* as Leo held her hand, walking around with her. Another walking lift, and Jess felt Leo's strong hands holding her as they moved together across the floor. The movement was effortless and poetic.

As they came to the end of the movement, the music faded. There was a moment's silence, then the assembled students and teachers in the room burst into applause. It was a wonderful moment, and Jess felt herself blush again.

She swept her eyes around and picked out Marco, who was applauding loudly. The girls playing the other two Muses were also applauding, no doubt wondering at how well they would now have to perform in order to try to match the same standard.

She saw Peter stood to one side, his bandana back on his head. She smiled at him and he smiled back at her encouragingly.

Jess grinned. She was very pleased with how she had danced. No faults at all as far as she could tell. But the tutors could always find something to pull you up on, and indeed Madame Rossi was stepping forward, smiling.

'Very good, Jess and Leo. Very good. Now. Some notes, and then we will go again …'

As Madame Rossi started pointing out to Leo where some of his movements had been a little out of sync with the music, and where perhaps more of a lightness was needed, Jess stretched her legs out on the wall bars. Her eyes caught a glimpse of someone in the shadows by the exit door, and her heart caught. Was it her stranger? She craned her neck to look past the other students, but all she could see was the door closing silently on its weighted hinge. Whoever had been there had just left the room. She looked quickly around, and realised that neither Marco nor Peter were in sight. Had they just left? She frowned inwardly and returned to the rest of the group. It wouldn't do to be caught daydreaming by Madame Rossi at this point.

'Anthony, Anthony! Some amazing news!' Jess called as she spotted her friend later that evening.

Anthony was carrying a bucket of water, but not without difficulty, as his leg seemed to be playing him up again.

'Let me help you with that,' offered Jess, taking the bucket from him.

Anthony smiled gratefully. 'Thanks Jess. It's a little hard sometimes …' He patted his leg with his free arm. 'It comes and goes,' he explained. 'I think it's something to do with the weather.'

'Let me tell you my news,' said Jess as she walked beside him. He held the door to the kitchen open for her, then limped along beside her.

'I've got the lead!'

'The lead? That's amazing!' said Anthony, obviously very pleased for her.

'Yes. Because of what happened to Rowan, Miss Rossi felt that I should take over. So I am dancing Calliope in *Appollon Musagete*! It's fantastic!'

'So all those nights of extra training helped?'

'Oh yes,' said Jess. 'It really made all the difference. I feel so strong and ready to do this now. Before, I was a bit of a mess …'

'No …'

'Yes I was, Anthony. And I need to thank you for being there for me.'

'What, me?' said Anthony. 'I didn't do anything … I just wanted to be your friend. I don't have many friends here.'

'Yes, you,' said Jess, playfully poking him with her finger. 'You listened to me, and I can talk to you … Don't underestimate that.'

She smiled fondly at him. 'So where does this go?' she asked, hefting the bucket.

'Oh, sorry, over there.' He gestured with his stick to the sink.

Jess hauled the bucket over there and, checking with Anthony, poured the contents out into the sink and down the drain.

'There's always something to mop up or clean down,' he said.

'Anyway,' said Jess. 'Thanks for being you.'

'A pleasure,' said Anthony. 'So what now? I guess your training must really ramp up a notch or two.'

'I thought that as well,' said Jess. 'And I think I also need to find out just who my masked man is … I mean, it's eating me up not knowing!'

Anthony looked thoughtful. 'Do you think that's wise? I mean, if you find out, then the game might be up and you might never see him again.'

Jess looked pained. 'I know,' she said. 'I'd thought of that. But he seems so nice … I just have to know.'

'Well, be careful,' said Anthony. 'When are you seeing him again?'

'I don't know yet,' said Jess as she held the kitchen door for Anthony. As they emerged into the public corridor, she kissed him on the cheek. 'I'll let you know.'

With that, she hurried away to her next lesson, the last of the day. It was time for another session with her man, and she was hopeful he would text her before the day was out. She pulled her mobile from her bag and ran her fingers over the screen. He'd better text her, anyway …

16

Jess lay back on her bed and moaned loudly as the tongue flickered across her sensitive clitoris again. She spread her legs as wide as they could go, and ran her hands over the slicked back hair of the stranger who was again servicing her.

He ran his hands over her stomach, and buried his face in her pussy, gently sucking and licking her.

She trembled and cried out as her orgasm built and built. It felt as though she was being turned inside out by her skilled lover as he eased back every time she thought she was about to cum. Teasing her with his tongue, and then pressing closer when she had moved back from the brink.

This just had the desired effect of bringing her to the brink even faster the next time, but he kept her trembling there, teetering on the moment of an intense orgasm, before easing her back once more.

'No … no … not fair …' she gasped after the third or fourth time, her hands clutching at the bedclothes and her hips twisting to try and get to the point of no return.

The stranger said nothing but continued his stimulation, running his tongue round and round her sensitive nub, sending sparks of pleasure through her body to her brain.

Jess needed him in her. Her pussy was aching to be filled, but the intense feelings were making it hard for her to think.

She felt a slightly different feeling. Something was gently probing and pressing against her opening. She gasped as the walls of her pussy were eased apart by a long finger, which penetrated her gently and started to caress and rub deep inside her.

Jess gasped and moaned, her head thrashing from side to side as the pleasure rapidly mounted again. His clever tongue lapped and caressed her clitoris while his finger massaged her pussy.

This was heaven!

Jess felt herself climbing again, getting higher and higher and closer and closer … the feelings all merging into a centre deep inside her. A place that just needed one more … one more …

'Oh … oooooohhhhh …'

The pleasure climaxed, and Jess's body jerked and spasmed uncontrollably as she came all over the man's tongue and finger. Her pussy ineffectually tried to grip onto the finger as she flooded it with her juices, orgasming again and again.

Her brain shut down temporarily and her hands gripped the sheets, knuckles white as her whole body tensed with the extreme pleasure.

At that moment she would have agreed to anything, done anything, just to continue in this state of arousal.

The stranger lifted his head from where he had been working his magic, and if she could have seen him, she would have seen him smile.

His finger continued gently to stroke her for a few moments, keeping her cumming again and again, until he slowly slid it from her. Jess started to come down from the intense feelings, and felt a wave of total languor wash over her.

Fuck, she thought. *This is how to relax after a long day. Forget the hot baths and the scrubbing with flannels ... this is how I want to end every day!*

She forced herself to breathe again, realising that she had been panting and making little squealing noises as she had cum her brains out. A part of her worried what her neighbours thought, but then she remembered how she had been treated to the symphony of banging headboards on her wall, and moans and cries of pleasure. Before, she had gone into a sulk, clenching her hands between her legs and wishing that it had been her on the receiving end ... Well ... now this was payback.

She smiled at the thought. *Let them wonder who it was fucking me so well!* She almost laughed out loud at that point. *Fuck ... I don't even know myself!*

She relaxed back into the bed and smiled down at her lover. He was watching her intently through the mask, his eyes glittering in the candlelight. She raised her arms to him, and he pushed himself up and on top of her. Glancing down, Jess saw his amazing big dick, fully erect, bouncing down below.

The man positioned himself over her and grinned at her. 'Ready?' he asked.

Without waiting for an answer, the man pushed forward, and Jess felt the lips of her pussy pushed apart by his cock-head. His cock pushed forward, deep down into her, and she could feel every inch of him.

She gasped and opened her eyes wide, almost finding it difficult to believe what she was feeling.

He braced himself and pulled back, thrusting smoothly forward again.

In a moment he had set up a smooth, effective fucking motion, which drove his large penis deep into her wet and pulsating cunt over and over again.

The feeling sent Jess right over the top again, and urging him on at the top of her voice, she came hard and fast, her voice deteriorating into meaningless grunts as the power of speech left her. She collapsed back again, her fluids coating his big dick as he continued to make love to her, keeping the feelings flooding her body.

She held his neck, opening her eyes to see his masked face above her. She tightened her muscles and gripped his member, trying to milk him for all she was worth.

After a few moments, he grunted and sped up slightly. Jess knew this meant he was close, so she stroked his chest, running her hands up and circling his nipples with her fingers. He moaned, and suddenly she was aware of her pussy being pumped full of cum. His big cock slowed, and he collapsed down onto her as he came.

She held him tight, gently stroking his back as he recovered. She was also feeling very relaxed, and so closed her eyes, loving the feeling of this man on top of her. She thought she would like to get used to this … but she had to find out who he was.

To this end, she had formulated a plan earlier in the evening.

When he had texted her to give the location for the evening's tryst, she had replied with, 'I'D PREFER MY ROOM,' to which, after a minute or so, had come the response, 'OK.'

Jess intended to follow the stranger after they had

finished and see where he went. That way she might be able to get closer to finding out who he really was.

The man pulled out of her and lay on his back, his breathing returning to normal. She lay beside him, one hand gently stroking his chest.

'You okay?' she asked.

The stranger looked at her through his mask. 'I'm good,' he said with a smile. 'You always make me feel good, Jess.'

Jess felt a warm glow in her chest when he said that. She loved it when he complimented her, and felt that perhaps this was one of the reasons why she had fallen for him.

After about five more minutes, he pushed himself up off the bed and started putting his clothes back on. Jess watched him. She liked watching him dress. He had a great body, well proportioned and athletic in a way that only dancers could develop. She tried to match his body with that of one of the boys in the Acadamie, but she couldn't. They all looked pretty similar.

Once he had all his clothes on, he smiled at Jess, bade her goodnight and moved to the door.

'Until next time,' she said.

With a mock bow, he opened the door and left.

Like a shot, Jess was up and off the bed. She threw on her robe, which she had positioned for easy access on her chair, and raced to the door. She opened it gently and peeked out, seeing the man's back moving away from her down the corridor.

She left her room and crept after him, keeping to the shadows between the other students' doorways. He turned at the end of the corridor and headed for the staircase. Jess followed, her feet scrunching quietly on the carpet.

When she got to the stairs, she looked up and saw the man just heading onto the floor above hers. She raced up the marble stairs and peeked into the corridor.

He was opening one of the doors. When he had entered, she hurried down the corridor and stopped by the door. It was ajar.

Furthermore, she knew the room. It was Marco's! She had been there a couple of times to deliver some letters when put on mail duties in her first year.

She swallowed and silently pushed the door open a little further. Through the gap she could see the full-length mirror that all the students had, and in it the reflection of her stranger. He was stood still, facing the other part of the room.

So, her lover was Marco! Jess found that she liked the thought of this.

Just then, the man moved, and Jess saw him turn to face the mirror. He raised his hands and removed the mask.

Jess' eyes widened, and her jaw dropped.

It wasn't Marco!

Standing in Marco's room, reflected in the mirror, was the man she had just made love to. He was wearing the same clothes, and had the same slicked back hair. He was holding the same mask in his hand that she had come to love.

But it was Anthony!

Anthony put the mask on the dresser and moved away. There was no sign of the usual limp, but it was most certainly Anthony there in the room.

Jess bit her lip. Why had he deceived her? How could it be him?

She slowly moved away from the door and hurried back down the stairs to her own room.

She felt a little sick. All this time she had been confiding in Anthony, and he had been promising to watch her back and keep her safe … but he had been the man all along! She felt a little betrayed, but at the same time excited. She liked Anthony as well, and if he was the stranger, then that was okay, wasn't it? But no, the truth was, it felt a little strange. Anthony's persona, the friend she knew, was just as much a disguise as his mask had been. She didn't know him at all. Even the limp that appeared so natural was obviously fake.

As she lay on her bed, she decided that she would have to go further with this. Part of her was angry, another part truly excited. After all, Anthony had gone to an amazing amount of trouble in order to seduce her. She couldn't ignore the fact that he was also a superb dancer and teacher. She had learnt so much from him in the last few months, both sexually and creatively. Somehow she had also learnt that both of these things went hand in hand.

But what did Anthony gain from his espionage? Was it all just to get in her pants? Or did he really care? He was Leo's brother, after all. Maybe they were more alike than she had first realised.

Jess sighed. She was tired of games and wanted the truth now. She needed to force Anthony to reveal himself to her … and she thought she knew how to do it.

17

Jess was up early the next day. She wanted to get some things prepared in order to force Anthony into revealing himself to her.

Overnight she had thought it all through and realised that the feelings that she had for the stranger were very similar to those she had for Anthony – it was like the man was Jekyll and Hyde: one half best friend, confidante and companion; and the other teacher, muse and lover. With the realisation that both were in fact the same person, Jess knew that she was right in wanting to make Anthony see that he couldn't continue to hide from her. She realised that she couldn't have been happier if the masked man had been anyone else. Anthony was her friend. Maybe his disguise had something to do with his own hang-ups. Jess felt ashamed that she had spent so much time telling Anthony her problems, but hardly knew anything about his.

She showered and dressed and headed down to the stage area to prepare her plan.

It was early and the stage was dark and gloomy at this hour, but she knew her way well enough.

Jess headed for the understage door that led to the

section where all the old props and costumes were stored. It was dusty and spidery there, and the ceiling – in fact the underside of the stage floor – was low so that she had to walk in a crouch to avoid banging her head.

She found what she was looking for and arranged her trap carefully – she had no wish to hurt herself with what she was planning. Giving it all a final check, she operated the lever that worked the stage trapdoor. A square of the ceiling hinged down and weak light filtered in from above.

She got under the door and manually lifted it onto her back. When it was back in position, she jammed a piece of card in between the door and the edge of the stage. When she had done this, and was happy it was secure, she carefully moved her body out of the way. The door remained closed, held in place by the piece of card.

Jess nodded to herself. That would have to do. She then headed off to the canteen for breakfast.

'Anthony!'

Jess called out to her friend when she saw him after breakfast. He was hobbling along with his stick as usual, some old curtains over his arm. Jess couldn't resist smiling. He was really good at pretending he had a problem ...

'Hi Jess. How's it going today?'

Jess thought he sounded a little tired. Whenever she had noticed that in the past she had always put it down to the work he did around the place, at all hours, and with a bad leg to contend with as well. Now that she knew he was also putting in extracurricular activity with her ... well, she had a new respect for his stamina!

'I'm good,' she grinned at him. 'I was wondering if

I could ask a favour?'

'You know me,' he said. 'Happy to help if I can.'

'It's a little embarrassing,' she said. 'You know the ballet that we're all rehearsing for …'

Anthony nodded. 'It's that *Apollo* thing isn't it?'

'*Appollon Musagete*, yes. Well, I'm worried about the positioning on the stage … It's all very well rehearsing in the dance studios, but the stage is very different … I was wondering if you might come and be my "audience", so you can tell me if it works?'

Anthony thought for a moment. 'I guess I can do that … When did you have in mind?'

Jess smiled at him gratefully. 'Well, I have a free hour now, if you're not tied up with something else. And I think the stage is free this morning.' *In fact, I know the stage is free, because I checked yesterday*, thought Jess.

'Okay then,' said Anthony. 'Give me five minutes to get rid of this, and I'll meet you in the auditorium.'

Jess watched Anthony head off to the storeroom, limping as usual and using his stick. She smiled, and hoped to hell that she was right …

Jess was waiting on the stage as Anthony entered the auditorium. She had switched on the house lights so that she could see what she was doing, and the place was bathed in their white glow.

'Hiya,' greeted Anthony. 'So where do you want me?'

Jess gestured to the middle of the centre block of seats. 'How about there? I just want to make sure that the people who pay a premium get the best view.'

Anthony nodded and made his way slowly along the row of seats to get to the middle one. He rested his stick on the seats beside him and sat down.

'Here okay?'

Jess nodded. 'Perfect!'

Jess moved back onto the stage and took up a position near the middle, around where her variation would actually start. She pulled off her baggy sweat-top and threw it to one side.

She swallowed, and tried not to look at the open trapdoor over to the left, pretending that she hadn't seen it.

'This is going to be without music,' she called to Anthony. 'So it might be a little rough, but I'm sure you'll get the idea.'

Anthony nodded in response and settled down in the seat.

Jess started with a *plié*, then moved into a slow sequence of steps across the stage. She stopped close to the edge of the trapdoor, then returned across the stage. She could see Anthony watching her closely, tapping his hand on the arm of the chair to the imagined beat of the music.

She smiled at him and continued with the movements, which were now very familiar to her indeed.

She crossed the stage again, and plucked up courage as she approached the trapdoor. She would have to do this just right.

As she neared it, she made a little jump, and landed dead in the centre of the trapdoor. The roll of card with which she had secured it gave way, and the floor vanished beneath her feet. She fell, and as she did so, she cried out in alarm.

'Jess!'

She heard Anthony shout out and race to the stage

– any pretence at a limp now gone. He vaulted up onto the stage and ran to where the open trapdoor was hanging.

Jess saw him appear over the lip, concern etched across his face.

'Jess! Are you okay? What happened?'

Jess saw his eyes flick from her to the pile of mattresses she had landed on.

'I'm fine,' she said. 'Thank goodness these were here!'

She struggled to her feet and raised a hand to Anthony.

'Can you help me out?'

He took her by the hand and hauled her up out of the pit with ease. She steadied herself on her feet and looked Anthony in the eyes.

'Thanks,' she said, and then looked down at his leg.

'I think you forgot something,' she said.

Anthony looked puzzled. 'Forgot something?'

Jess nodded and gestured over to the seats, where his stick was still lying in view where he had left it.

'Your stick?'

Anthony looked over to where it was lying and then back at Jess. 'I … I … I thought you might be hurt,' he said.

Jess smiled at him. 'I'm fine,' she said. 'But I think we have something to talk about.'

Anthony was silent and looked at her face. He could see that the truth was out, and nothing he could say would change that.

'I'm sorry,' he managed.

'I'm not,' said Jess. 'And Anthony, if you've not guessed by now, I am, in fact, very much in love with you.'

It was Anthony's turn to blush, and Jess smiled and kissed him gently on the cheek.

'Come on, you. We have some talking to do.'

And with that she turned and they helped each other down and off the stage.

Anthony collected his stick as they left the auditorium. 'I guess I'd better,' he said. 'Otherwise other people might start asking questions as well.'

Jess nodded, and led the way back to her room where they could talk in private.

18

Jess handed Anthony a cup of whisky and sat down on the bed beside him, her own cup cradled in her hands.

'I always keep some of this,' she explained, as Anthony sniffed the drink cautiously. 'You never know when you might need a little tot after a long day.'

Anthony smiled and sipped at the alcohol.

'So,' said Jess. 'Tell me what all this is about.'

Anthony shook his head and looked into his drink. 'I don't even know where to start,' he said.

'How about with the leg and the stick,' said Jess. 'What's the deal with the limp?'

'Well, you know that Leo is my brother,' he began, 'and that once I hurt my leg, Leo took every opportunity he could to ridicule me, deride me and put me down. Time after time I would find that Leo had "arranged" some activity in which I couldn't be included. It just wasn't fair.

'Even more so because I was the one who had actually worked with and trained my little brother. Leo was no more than a passable dancer before I took him under my wing and trained with him, shaped him, got him as good as I could get him.'

Jess watched Anthony intently as he spoke. His voice was soft, but she could hear the hurt and pain in his words.

'It was I who managed to get us both a placement at the Acadamie. I filled in all the application forms myself, as Leo was too busy flirting with the ladies to be bothered with that sort of thing. We both did well to start with, then one day during training I landed wrongly on my foot and it just sort of crumpled below me, twisting and tearing the ligaments in my leg. I was in plaster for three months, and then had to learn how to walk again. It took ages!

'I got used to using the stick, and meanwhile Leo had advanced in leaps and bounds – excuse the pun – and was the toast of the Acadamie. All I could think of was to help out however I could, so I offered to do some of the general odd jobs about the place, and the Acadamie board were gracious enough to let me. I think they felt a little guilty that I had started there as a dancer, but now seemed to have no future in that direction.'

'But you're a great dancer!' Jess said.

'Thanks. The problem I had really was Leo. He had a habit of "forgetting" when anyone asked him where he had trained, or who had helped him. It really irritated me. That man had turned out to be such an idiot, arrogant and cocksure – not helped of course by all the girls who fell at his feet and fawned over him. Whenever he sees me, he is so disparaging. He thinks I'm useless, and so has basically discarded me. Which is the same thing he does to all those girls. I feel sorry for them.

'So I decided to fight back in the only way I could. I started to train in secret, strengthening my leg to the point that I no longer needed the stick. But it was a useful prop to explain why I was still at the Acadamie –

and of course my helping out with the odd jobs gave me access to all sorts of things that the rest of the students could not. I wasn't about to lose all that. So I maintained the limp and the stick … That way I could be invisible and go about my business unhindered, while all the time training and getting myself back to what I was before.'

Jess nodded. She understood about being invisible and what that felt like. She put her hand on his leg and rubbed it gently. 'I know,' she said.

'And then you came along,' he said, gazing into her eyes. 'I think I fell in love with you the first time I saw you. Your eyes, so blue and clear, and your talent, so undeveloped and yet so essential and vibrant.'

Jess blushed. No-one had ever said things like that to her before.

'But then, of course, there was Leo. He liked you too. Liked you a lot.'

'Did he?' exclaimed Jess. 'He never came on to me …'

'That's because he wanted you to do the running. He's used to that, you see. He likes the girls to chase him, so he can pick and choose who to fuck at any given point, and who to discard as it suits him. You were an enigma to him. You weren't interested in him, and so he just had to have you … but that wasn't going to happen.

'I think that made me fall in love with you even more, that you weren't like the other girls, that you were made of stronger stuff. And I decided that the best way to get back at Leo was to help you. To train you as I had done him all that time ago, to make you the best dancer I could.

'I even thought that maybe you would start to love me, but I was afraid. I was terrified that you might see me as everyone else did. Anthony the janitor, the invisible man. And why would you ever listen to me about dance or technique?

'So I devised my *alter ego*, the masked man, someone you could believe in and trust.'

'But I trusted you, Anthony! I talked to you, and shared secrets with you.'

'I know,' Anthony said quietly. 'And I realised then that you liked me, and that I wasn't invisible to you. But I couldn't reveal my past to you. I was worried that you might turn on me like everyone else.'

'Never!' said Jess.

'But you might have done. And then, as the masked man, I could love you as well. I thought you'd never want Anthony the cripple in the same way.'

Jess looked at Anthony sadly, and saw that he was hurting badly with these revelations. She knew that in a way he was right. That she had seen him as just a friend, and nothing more. But the masked man had excited her, and moved her. Knowing that they were one and the same person left her a little bewildered, but at least she was starting to understand Anthony's reasons for the deception, and they did make sense to her. Besides, she had always thought him attractive, although she would never have made any move to change the friendship they had.

'What I wasn't prepared for,' Anthony continued, 'was to fall in love with you so completely. Not being with you has been so painful. I've missed you so much.'

He bowed his head, and Jess saw a tear fall into his cup of whisky, making ripples.

'Oh Anthony,' she said. 'Come here.'

Jess took him in her arms and rocked him gently, stroking the back of his head. He drew in a ragged breath, and sniffled.

'I'm sorry,' he said. 'I must seem like a total idiot.'

Jess kissed his hair. 'No. Not at all.'

She kissed his forehead and chucked one hand under his chin. 'Look at me.'

Anthony raised his head and looked at her. His eyes were blurry with tears, and he obviously felt awful.

'You,' said Jess, with a kiss to his nose.

'Are,' with a kiss to his chin.

'Amazing,' with a kiss to his lips.

Anthony sniffed, and pulled back to look at her. 'You're not disappointed with me?'

Jess laughed. 'Disappointed? Far from it. You are the most incredible man!'

Anthony smiled. 'I've not let you down then?'

Jess shook her head slowly. 'No. And I think I know how I can show you.'

Anthony watched as she rose from the bed gracefully.

Fixing him with her eyes, she knelt before him, and gently started to help him off with his shirt. He allowed her to undress him. He stood and she slipped his trousers and boxers down, smiling when his member was revealed to her. Even flaccid he was a big boy.

She stood. 'Get into bed.'

Anthony scooted back and jumped into her bed, pulling the covers over him.

Jess made sure that the door to her room was locked, and turned to Anthony with a teasing smile on her face. She then slowly stripped off all her clothes. When her breasts bobbed into view, Anthony smiled, liking that the nipples were already hard with arousal.

She slid her leggings down, revealing her slim legs and shaved pussy. As she took her leggings off, Jess cheekily bent over, displaying her pert ass to Anthony.

When she was completely naked, she slid into bed beside Anthony, and ran her hand over his chest.

'This is nice,' she commented, gazing into his eyes, no longer looking at her from behind a mask.

Her hand stroked lower, and she found his cock. It stirred slightly in her hand and she smiled.

'Wonder what happens if I just …' and she dipped her head and gently lapped at one of his nipples. His cock immediately jerked and she could feel it getting larger.

'Mmmmm, lovely,' Jess murmured, and kissed Anthony on the mouth, her tongue parting his lips. He kissed her back, their tongues gently curling around each other. His hand went around the back of her head as they kissed, stroking her hair and holding her close.

When Jess could feel that Anthony's cock was nicely erect, she pushed him back onto the bed and threw the covers off. She scooted down his body, stroking and caressing him as she went, until her head was level with his cock. By now it was large and straining, and Jess ran her fingers up and down his length, marvelling at the size.

'You have a lovely cock, you know,' she said, looking up into his eyes. Then, without breaking eye contact, she slid her lips over his cock-head. Her tongue bathed him in saliva, and she started to slide her lips down on him.

Anthony closed his eyes in pleasure as she fellated him. It was the most amazing feeling. Jess's hot mouth covering his sensitive cock, and her tongue constantly moving against and around him, massaging him.

As she worked on his cock, Jess moved one of her hands to his balls, and gently scratched at them with her nails. She smiled around the member in her mouth as she felt Anthony tense under her.

She removed her lips from his penis with a pop. 'You like that, baby?' she asked innocently.

Anthony could only moan in response, as she immediately sucked his cock back into her mouth, her hand alternately stroking his shaft and fondling his balls.

Anthony was in heaven. He had never had a blow job so good before! Jess was making love to his dick like her life depended on it.

Anthony's breathing started to speed up as her ministrations were bringing him closer and closer to the edge. He moaned again, and squirmed under her.

Jess let his penis pop from her mouth again, and with a final stroke and lick, she released him.

'I can think of a much better place for that … can't you?' she asked.

Anthony looked her in the eyes. God, he loved this girl.

Jess moved so she was lying on the bed, and Anthony positioned himself over her. His penis was throbbing, and was larger than even he had ever seen it. *That's what the attentions of a good woman can do for you*, he thought.

Jess spread her legs as wide as she could. She was so wet and aroused and ready for Anthony. Even so, she gasped as his cock-head lodged itself into her opening and he moved forward. He was so big!

She bent her legs slightly and moaned as his shaft moved into her, filling her completely.

She opened her eyes to see Anthony above her, his smile in place. 'You like?' he asked.

Jess nodded. 'Very much – ooooohhh.'

Anthony had pulled out and then re-entered her smoothly, causing her to lose what she was saying.

He set up a steady fucking motion, pumping in and out of Jess's body. Balanced on one arm, he could kiss her, so they tenderly kissed as he made love to her. Stroking his dick in and out of her pussy. She was so wet that there was no resistance, and her pussy made tiny sucking noises each time he moved, as her muscles tried in vain to grip onto the large object that was making them twitch with pleasure.

Jess broke the kiss and arched her back as she came.

'Oh … oh … oh my God … yes … yes … yessssssss!'

Her hands flew down and clutched at the bedclothes as a huge orgasm was wrenched from her. Her breathing was ragged, and her pussy was on fire.

Anthony slowed slightly, and then, with the additional liquid inside her from her orgasm, started to fuck her faster and harder.

He could feel his own orgasm coming, his balls tightening and his shaft swelling in anticipation.

Jess cried out as she came again, trying to thrash on the bed beneath her, and the sudden clenching of her pussy caused Anthony to cum as well. He moaned as his cock unloaded spurt after spurt of hot cum into Jess. She loved the feel of it herself, and milked him with her muscles, feeling him relax as he completed his orgasm.

He collapsed down onto her, his cock still large inside her. She loved the feeling of being totally full and complete.

After a moment Anthony rolled off her and lay beside her. Her body was jerking slightly every so often from the aftershocks of the orgasms she had enjoyed, and she cuddled Anthony to her, looking down at his face, so happy and content.

He opened his eyes and looked into her face, seeing her flushed, but relaxed and happy. He thought she was the most beautiful thing he had ever seen.

Anthony sighed and snuggled into her. Jess held him close. Now they would never be parted.

19

The hallway was bustling with people as Jess and Anthony made their way down to breakfast.

Anthony was still walking with his stick. He had explained to Jess that he thought he ought to maintain the façade at least for the moment. Otherwise people might start to ask questions. He could ease off on the use of it over the coming weeks, and explain that his leg had finally started to heal enough for him to walk unaided. After that, he could restart training and dancing at the Acadamie.

Jess thought that he could probably apply for a teaching post, he was that good, but again this would come in time.

As they turned one of the corners, Jess passed by Natalie and her cronies, who stood there watching her. They started whispering to each other.

'What is their problem!' said Jess to Anthony.

'No idea,' he replied. 'But whatever it is, it's not your problem. Let them play their games and whisper their secrets. It's you who is dancing the lead in the ballet and not them.'

Jess smiled. Deep down she knew this, but with

Anthony stating the obvious to her, it seemed to make it all okay.

They arrived at the canteen and Jess went to get a tray of food for them, while Anthony snagged a table – he found it tricky to balance walking with a stick and carrying a tray.

While she was waiting in the queue, Jess felt a hand on her arm.

'Hi Jess.'

It was Marco. She turned and smiled at him. 'Oh, hi Marco. How's things today?'

'Good, thanks,' he said. Then he leaned towards her conspiratorially. 'I wanted to ask you something … about Anthony.'

Jess's heart sank. Had the gossip got out already? This place was awful. She shot a panicked look at Anthony, seated at the table waiting for her. He could see that Marco was talking to her, and an expression of enquiry crossed his face.

'What about Anthony?' she asked, thinking that the best way to deal with this would be to play dumb.

'Well … I know you're friends with him, right?'

Jess nodded, wondering where this was going.

'Well … you see … I kinda like him. If you know what I mean? And I was wondering if … well, if he was … into guys … and was dating anyone at the moment? It's kinda hard for me to ask him direct …'

Jess burst into explosive laughter in the queue. She just couldn't help it. She calmed herself down.

'Oh, I'm sorry Marco, I'm sorry,' she put her hand on his arm. 'That must have sounded all wrong. It's not you, I'm just … it's just …' She cleared her throat and composed herself. 'I'm really sorry. Anthony isn't into boys.'

Marco's face fell and Jess felt sorry for him.

'Don't worry, there are plenty of others who are.' She cast her eyes around the canteen and spotted a group of lads at the back. She barely knew them, but she did know that one of them was gay – this fact had come to light earlier in the year at one of the social evenings.

'Why not go and sit with them?' she gestured. 'You never know … you might make some new friends.'

Marco smiled at her. 'Thanks Jess,' he said. 'And … you won't mention this to anyone, will you? I mean about Anthony?'

'Don't worry,' she said. 'Your secret is safe with me.'

Marco nodded his thanks and headed off with his tray to sit with the lads. Jess watched him go, a smile on her face. All this time and she had thought that Marco had the hots for her, when it was Anthony that he had been checking out. Just goes to show that you can't judge people. You never know what they might really be thinking.

She headed back to Anthony with a couple of breakfast rolls and some orange juice. She felt giddy and happy inside. Fulfilled and content.

All she had ever wanted was to have a boyfriend to love and support her, and to succeed in her training as a dancer, and her dream had come true. She looked around at the canteen, and silently thanked the Acadamie for everything it had brought her.

She sat and gazed into the eyes of her lover.

Life was good.

CODA – THREE MONTHS LATER

The *Ballet dell Italia*'s performance of *Appollon Musagete* was drawing to a conclusion.

On stage, the dancers were performing *Apotheosis*, the final act in the piece.

As with previous stagings of this ballet, all the outfits were in clean white, and the stage dressings and settings were minimal. All designed to emphasise and highlight the music and the dance.

The main characters were on stage centre: Leo and Jess dancing Apollo and Calliope respectively. Around them were the other two Muses, Polyhymnia and Terpsichore, and behind them was Marco as Hades, along with a group of Chorus dancers representing the various elements of Mount Parnassus.

As Stravinsky's elegant music soared and filled the auditorium, so Jess and Leo performed the final steps.

Jess tiptoed across the stage *en pointe*, arms held up, and fell into Leo's arms. He effortlessly glided her around, and she sprang from him as though on elastic, making an impressive leap to land in a *plié* before continuing the movement across the stage, taking a full spin with every step so that her smiling face was always turned to the audience.

Then she made a run back toward Leo and gracefully leaped into his arms, where he held her for a moment before dropping to one knee and releasing her once more.

Then the climactic leap from Apollo.

Leo stepped back and away and prepared for his run. Jess was ready for him. He ran, jumped, twisted. Jess was in exactly the right spot, as had been rehearsed and rehearsed, and she provided the small lift needed to propel Leo over her head, twisting, to land faultlessly beyond her.

As the music and ballet reached its conclusion, the three Muses left Apollo and Hades and took their place on Parnassus, the end of their journey.

There was a moment of silence as the ballet ended and the music stopped, but then the auditorium erupted in a cacophony of applause.

Jess could hardly believe it had gone so perfectly. She and the other dancers made their way to the front of the stage to take their bow.

She looked out into the audience and could see that they were all on their feet, applauding loudly. There were some whistles and shouts too.

First Leo took a solo bow, the applause not diminishing as he did so.

Then it was Jess's turn, and as she performed a deep curtsey to the crowd, so it erupted in even louder cheers and applause. They went wild.

Jess saw some roses being thrown onto the stage in front of her, and a child hurried on from the wings carrying a bouquet of flowers.

Her eyes were streaming with tears. All this was for her.

She curtseyed again, releasing even more howls of appreciation from the audience.

Jess looked around at the company, and all were stood on the stage applauding her. Even Leo was shaking his head in admiration and smiling and applauding.

She looked to the wings.

And there she could see Anthony, now without his stick, smiling and with tears rolling down his face, applauding her as hard as he could.

ABOUT THE AUTHOR

Athena Michaels lives in London with her husband John and their two cats Ben and Jerry.

OTHER TITLES BY TELOS

MOONRISE

Sinful Pleasures

Byte Me! by Roberta Steele
Lady of Witchcraven by Kate Daniels

Romantic Encounters

Helen McCabe
The Price of Love
Love in Hiding
In Search of Love
Hostage to Love
When Love Rides Out
Highway of Fear
A Garden Fair
The House on the Mountain

Juliette Benzoni
Catherine: One Love is Enough
Catherine
Belle Catherine
Catherine and Arnaud
Catherine and a Time for Love
A Snare for Catherine
The Lady of Montsalvy